P9-BIJ-883

Her stories of love's special magic
made her a NATIONAL BESTSELLING AUTHOR...

The Matchmaker, Star-Crossed Lovers, and two delightful
love stories in one special book,
Kissed by Magic/Belonging to Taylor...now

KAY HOOPER

reveals the uncertainty in every new lover's
heart—and the ecstasy of the passion that awaits...

ELUSIVE DAWN

"Robyn, you're playing with fire," Shane warned hoarsely.

She gasped at the feel of his thumb probing through the
material of her knit top, and she managed to say fiercely,
breathlessly, "I hope I get burned!"

Quite suddenly, her upper arms were gripped in steely hands,
and she was held nearly a foot away from the body she wanted
so badly to touch.

"But *I* don't want to be the one to burn you. Don't you understand that?" he asked hoarsely. "I don't want to wake up in the
morning and find you gone because you only needed one night.
I need *more* than one night, dammit! And until I'm sure—"

Robyn broke the grip of his hands and took a careful step
backward. For the first time, she was furious with him. He was
trying to back her into a corner, and she didn't like it one bit!

Also by Kay Hooper from Jove

KISSED BY MAGIC/BELONGING TO TAYLOR

ELUSIVE DAWN

KAY HOOPER

**Originally published under
the pseudonym Kay Robbins**

JOVE BOOKS, NEW YORK

If you purchased this book without a cover, you should be aware that this book is stolen property. It was reported as "unsold and destroyed" to the publisher, and neither the author nor the publisher has received any payment for this "stripped book."

This Jove Book contains the complete
text of the original edition.
It has been completely reset in a typeface
designed for easy reading and was printed
from new film.

ELUSIVE DAWN

A Jove Book / published by arrangement with
the author

PRINTING HISTORY
Originally appeared as Second Chance at Love
title *Elusive Dawn* / March 1983
Jove edition / September 1993

All rights reserved.
Copyright © 1983 by Kay Robbins a.k.a. Kay Hooper.
Cover photograph by Wendi Schneider.
This book may not be reproduced in whole or in part,
by mimeograph or any other means, without permission.
For information address: The Berkley Publishing Group,
200 Madison Avenue, New York, New York 10016.

ISBN: 0-515-11187-2

Jove Books are published by The Berkley Publishing Group,
200 Madison Avenue, New York, New York 10016.
The name "JOVE" and the "J" logo
are trademarks belonging to Jove Publications, Inc.

PRINTED IN THE UNITED STATES OF AMERICA

10 9 8 7 6 5 4 3 2 1

For Beth . . .
the niece born while
this book was being written.

CHAPTER
One

THE PARTY HAD been going on for nearly an hour, and Robyn was numb from the music and laughter. Vaguely, she wondered where Kris was, and wondered again why she had allowed her cousin to talk her into coming. She had never been very good at parties anyway, and the past year had quite effectively destroyed her ability to laugh.

She was looking around, trying to find her cousin, when a face across the room suddenly caught her attention. It was a hard face in many ways, the planes and angles of it strong and proud, the features roughly hewn and magnetically attractive. And there was something familiar about that face ... something hauntingly familiar.

The man looked up and saw her just then, his eyes first widening and then narrowing as they took in her slender figure poised as if for flight. Without so much as a word to the other man at his side, he crossed the room in a few long strides, halting before her to stare down into her dazed eyes.

"Hello," he murmured, a peculiar huskiness in his deep voice.

Robyn stared up at him, only dimly realizing that he was taller than she had first supposed, topping her by a head in spite of her high heels. "Hello," she whispered, barely conscious of the people and noise now, feeling that she was drowning in the darkening green pools of his eyes.

"Dance with me."

It wasn't a request, and Robyn didn't even question her own desire to be in this man's arms. The music had changed to a slow, sensuous beat, and she felt it entering her body, keeping pace with her heart and the blood rushing through her veins as he led her out onto the cleared space reserved for dancing. With no attempt to be coy, she drifted into his arms naturally, eagerly, feeling his hands at her waist, his breath stirring the hair piled loosely on top of her head. Their steps matched perfectly.

"You're a little thing," he murmured, his large hands easily spanning her waist. "I could almost put you in my pocket and steal you away from whoever brought you tonight." His voice was still husky, low, and intimate.

Silently, dreamily, Robyn allowed her body to mold itself pliantly to his, her hands moving naturally to his shoulders. Her trembling fingers began to stroke the dark hair on the nape of his neck. She was aware of his hands moving slowly over her back, which was left bare by her shimmering aqua dress. She rested her forehead against his crisp white shirt, feeling a pulse pounding and not sure whether it was hers or his.

"You're not real!" he breathed suddenly, pulling her lower body against him fiercely. Their steps were so slow they were very nearly dancing in place. "I dreamed you. I've always dreamed you."

She wished vaguely that he wouldn't talk, would leave her alone to live in her own dream. She felt so safe, so content in a world where pain and tragedy were unheard of.

"Tell me your name," he commanded softly, and when she didn't respond, one of his hands slid down her arm to the delicate silver identification bracelet on her slender wrist, his thumb toying with the tiny charms and then brushing across the name engraved in flowing script. "Robyn?"

She lifted her head at last, nodding slightly as her eyes met his. The music had changed again to a faster beat, but they continued to dance slowly, completely wrapped up in each other and totally oblivious to anything else.

"Robyn," he murmured, the deep voice turning her name into a caress. "It suits you—something small and fragile." He brushed his lips across her forehead and added, "My name's Shane."

Robyn pushed the information aside. It didn't belong in her dream. But his desire did. She could feel his urgency in the tightening muscles of his strong body, could feel the need he made no effort to hide, and it matched her own need. There was an ache in her body which, she somehow knew, could only be assuaged by this man's touch.

She would lose herself in the dream. For this one night, she would forget everything that had gone before.

She looked up at him through long, thick lashes, and her lips parted in instant response as he bent his head to kiss her. She held nothing back, made no attempt to insist on the slow building of passion that was an ages-old rule in the mating game. She felt his lips moving on hers, at first gentle and then demanding.

He made a soft but rough sound deep in his throat, his eyes gleaming with the hard shine of raw emeralds as he drew back far enough to gaze down at her. "Let's get out of here," he muttered hoarsely. "I want to do more than just hold you in my arms."

Robyn followed as he led her from the room, barely noticing the startled faces of the other guests. She had forgotten her cousin, her eyes fixed intently on the man whose hand she held tightly.

He turned in the entrance hall of the apartment, looking down at her almost impatiently. "Did you have a wrap?"

"No," she murmured. "But my purse . . ." She left him standing there while she went into a small room off the hall and located her handbag. Stepping back into the hall, she suddenly heard her cousin's worried voice.

"Robyn?"

She half pivoted, staring toward the doorway of the den where her cousin stood. Kris's eyes were concerned, a faintly shocked expression gripping her Florida-golden features.

For a moment, a tiny split second, the dream cracked and allowed reality to seep in. But Robyn knew just how brutal reality could be, and she preferred her dream. Waving good-bye and turning her back on her worried cousin, she walked steadily across the hall and put her hand with absolute trust into Shane's.

His eyes flared oddly, and he made another one of

those strange, rough sounds under his breath, carrying her hand to his lips briefly before leading her from the apartment.

He put his arm around her in the elevator, holding her close to his side, and Robyn cuddled up to him like a sleepy kitten. She felt safe, at home; nothing else mattered. She only dimly noticed the luxury of the black Porsche he tucked her into a few moments later.

The Miami night was hot, still, almost waiting, just as she waited for them to reach their destination. She half turned on the seat, watching Shane's profile, bemused and bewildered by the strength of her own need. She didn't remember that; it wasn't part of the dream. But then, it had been so long.

He handled the powerful car easily as they crossed the bay into Miami Beach, weaving it among the late-night traffic common in this tourist city of hotels and night spots. At last the car drew to a stop in front of one of the more luxurious hotels, and he got out and came around to open her door even before the doorman could reach them. Again, Robyn put her hand in his with complete trust and assurance, silently following him into the building.

Five minutes later he was closing the door of the penthouse suite, leaning back against it and watching as she wandered into the sunken living room. She looked at the ultra-modern furnishings, the abstracts on the walls, the ocean view from a row of floor-to-ceiling windows. None of it really registered. Only the man did.

She turned to look at him. What was he waiting for? Did he think she expected the ritual drink, casual conversation. That would be a waste of precious time; they had only tonight. With simple directness, she asked, "Do you want me?"

He slowly pushed himself away from the door, walking toward her as if in a daze, the emerald eyes glowing. "Oh, yes," he breathed, halting before her. "I want you very much."

Robyn dropped her purse onto a chair and stepped closer to him, her arms slipping up around his neck. "Then what are you waiting for?" she asked softly.

He caught his breath sharply, bending to swing her into his arms and striding down the short, carpeted hallway to the bedroom. The room was lit only by moonlight when he carried her in, but after setting her gently on her feet, he reached to turn on a lamp on the night table, casting a soft glow over them and the huge bed.

"Do you mind?" he asked huskily. "I want to look at you."

"No," she murmured, surprising herself by adding honestly, "I want to look at you, too."

His eyes darkened to a mysterious shade that Robyn found completely fascinating, and she could only gaze into those pools, lose herself in them, as his head bent slowly toward her.

His lips touched hers lightly, teasingly, feathering gentle kisses from one corner of her mouth to the other. His hands were expertly unfastening the clasp of her dress, sliding the zipper down. The dress slid to the floor with a mere whisper of sound, and Robyn stood before him clad only in the skimpiest of bras and delicate white panties.

The strange rumble came again from the depths of his chest, and she tried vaguely to identify it as she stared up into his brilliant eyes. The sound reminded her of something, but what? And then she had it: the curious sound was very like the throaty, rumbling purr of a contented lion.

"Undress me," he whispered hoarsely, guiding her hands to the buttons of his shirt. He shrugged from the casual jacket as she willingly complied with the request, her slender fingers moving nimbly from one button to another, her eyes still fixed with almost painful intensity on his face. She pushed the shirt from his broad, tanned shoulders, her fingers lingering for a moment to explore the corded strength of his neck and then sliding slowly down the hair-roughened chest to find the belt riding low on his hips. With unconscious familiarity, she unfastened the belt and then the zipper, pushing the pants down over his narrow hips.

Obviously losing patience with the time-consuming task, he groaned softly and brushed her hands aside, rapidly removing the remainder of his garments. Robyn watched unself-consciously, stepping out of her high-heeled sandals and kicking them aside.

She was astonished at the beauty of his lean body, oddly moved by the tremor of his hands and the naked longing in his eyes. He looked at her the way a starving man might gaze at a feast, she mused to herself, and she was dimly troubled by that. But then he reached out for her again, and she forgot the disturbing image.

His large hands smoothed away her delicate underthings with gentle roughness until at last she stood as nude as he. With a strange catch in his voice, he groaned, "God, but you're beautiful!" One hand rose to cup a small, full breast, his thumb teasing until a nipple rose to taut awareness.

Robyn gasped, her arms sliding up around his neck and her fingers thrusting fiercely into his thick black hair. She needed him so desperately. She rose on tiptoe to fit herself more firmly against the hard length of him. He crushed her to him for a moment, then swept her up and placed her gently on the bed, apparently too impatient to strip away the plush velvet spread.

Robyn didn't mind; she scarcely even noticed. She held out her arms to him as he lowered his weight beside her, and the green eyes flared again with some fleeting emotion she didn't try to identify. Green... his eyes were green. It was a jarring note in her dream. She closed her own eyes and made his blue.

She felt his fingers in her hair, releasing the pins and smoothing the waist-length silky mass over the velvet-covered pillows.

"A siren," he rasped, a peculiar shivering moan in his deep voice. "A raven-haired witch." His lips lowered to drop hot kisses on first one breast and then the other, teasing and tormenting each throbbing nipple in turn. "Such a tiny witch to possess such power..."

"Power?" she asked throatily, her fingers kneading his muscle-padded shoulders, her eyes flickering open in curiosity.

He laughed huskily, lifting his head to stare down at her with green flames in his eyes. "Power," he confirmed softly. "Don't you know, sweet witch, what you do to me? Can't you feel the fire in me—the fire you started? The fire only you can extinguish?"

Robyn trailed one hand down his back, letting him feel the gentle scratch of her long nails, and experiencing, indeed, a strange sense of power when he shuddered and groaned. "Am I putting out the fire?" she teased softly, watching the flames in his green eyes leap even higher.

"No!" he grated, lowering his face to her throat and pressing feverish kisses on the soft, scented flesh there. His hands moved over her body urgently, possessively. "Oh, Robyn, love, I need you so badly! Go on touching me, sweetheart—don't ever stop!"

Robyn wondered briefly at the endearments, then decided that they fit her dream very well. Eagerly, she explored his body, entranced by the strength and heat of his desire. She moaned raggedly as his own fingers searched and probed, finding at last the heart of her quivering need and causing her body to arch almost convulsively against him.

She gasped aloud, dizzily aware of his erotic touch, of the exquisite tension filling her body, her consciousness. "Oh, please, Sh–Shane!" The name rose to her lips uncertainly, her voice trembling with intolerable desire.

With a low growl of answering male need, Shane rose above her, slipping between her trembling thighs and allowing her to feel his heavy weight for the first time. He came to her then. Came to her as though he intended to make her his for all time.

Robyn clung to him, moving with him, staggered by the feelings ripping through her body. The tension built higher and higher, an avid, primitive craving for satisfaction. She was keenly aware of his taut face above her, of digging her nails into his shoulders, and of pleading with him in an unfamiliar, drugged voice.

Then there was an eternal moment of shattering rapture, and she heard him groan her name hoarsely even as she cried out with the force of her release.

Silence reigned in the room for a long time as they lay in an exhausted tangle of arms and legs, hearts gradually returning to normal and breathing losing its ragged edge. It was Shane who finally broke the silence, and there was an unexpected spark of humor in his deep voice.

"Shall we get under the covers, or would you rather freeze in the air-conditioning?"

Robyn giggled sleepily. She was still firmly enmeshed in her dream, and she welcomed the humor that allowed her to resist reality a while longer.

"I gather that means you're leaving it up to me!" He gave a smothered laugh and then went through a series of complicated maneuvers designed to get them both under the covers without his losing his possessive hold on her.

By the time the feat was accomplished, Robyn was giggling even more. Shane drew her firmly into his arms, pulling the covers up around them and then reaching to turn off the lamp. "Don't laugh, witch— next time, I'll make *you* get the covers!" he warned with a deep chuckle.

Robyn snuggled up to him contentedly, feeling his hands stroking her long hair gently, his arms holding her tightly. Oh, God, it had been so long since she'd gone to sleep in a man's arms! If she pushed the dream a bit farther, she could almost believe . . .

"Robyn?"

"Ummm?" she murmured, her voice muffled against the warm flesh of his throat.

"We've skipped a few stops along the way; you realize that, don't you? We're going to have to talk in the morning."

"Ummm," she responded, determined to keep reality at bay just a bit longer.

He laughed softly and drew her even closer. "Go to sleep, honey," he murmured.

Robyn did just that, lulled by the steady sound of his heart beating, the curiously familiar warmth of his hard body against the softness of hers.

She woke in the gray morning hours, immediately aware of what had happened the night before and still reluctant to end her dream. But she had no choice. If she remained with this man . . . She moved cautiously to free herself from his loosened embrace, holding her breath when he muttered something and then turned his face into her pillow. Still cautious, she eased from the bed and dressed quickly in the aqua dress, her gaze turning again and again to the man sleeping in the huge bed.

Dressed, and aware of the lightening sky over the ocean, she still hesitated, staring at Shane. "Thank you," she breathed to the sleeping man. "You made me feel alive again. But I can't stay. It's better this way . . . a beautiful night to remember."

She didn't feel the least bit odd in standing there speaking softly to a sleeping man in a room filling with dawn light. She felt that she had to voice her thoughts. It seemed a fitting ending, somehow, to her dream.

"I only wish . . ."

The wistful whisper died away before she could form the thought fully in her own mind, and she was glad. Wishes too often didn't come true, and she wanted nothing to spoil the memory of her dream.

She slipped silently from the bedroom after a last, lingering glance at the man in the bed, retrieved her purse from the living room, and then left the suite. Her dress whispered softly around her ankles as she walked briskly to the elevator.

She found a cab outside the hotel and climbed in, giving the driver her address and then sitting back for the long ride across the bay. She realized absently that her hair was still loose, mussed from Shane's fingers, but she didn't bother doing anything about it.

The sun was hanging low in the eastern sky when her cab at last drew into the drive of her secluded home a few miles south of Miami. She paid the driver and watched him leave, then turned her gaze to the sprawling, Spanish-style house with its tile roof and mellow, sand-colored stucco finish. High hedges provided privacy, and tropical plants gave the place the look of someone's idea of paradise.

Abruptly, Robyn realized that the place was far too large for just one person—well, two, counting Marty. And, really, it wasn't as if it contained a lot of memories. She and Brian had traveled so much during that year; they had rarely been home, and never for very long.

She slowly moved up the walk, fishing her keys from her purse and silently questioning her decision to keep the house. Why not sell it and move somewhere else? Somewhere with definite seasons—snow up to her eyebrows in the winter! If it weren't for her store . . . Well, she could have another store, couldn't she?

Still arguing with herself, Robyn aimed the key at the lock, but it never quite connected. The door was pulled open suddenly, and a middle-aged woman with graying hair and a fierce frown on her face regarded Robyn sternly.

"So, you're finally home," she announced with awful politeness. "And just where have you *been* all night, Miss Robyn? Miss Kristina came by after that party last night and waited here for three hours; she was very upset with you!"

"And you aren't?" Robyn murmured dryly, stepping inside and closing the door firmly behind herself.

The older woman gave a sniff of disdain as she stared at Robyn's rumpled dress and loose hair. "Coming in with the sun and looking like something the cat dragged in!"

"That's enough, Marty," Robyn said mildly.

She was ignored. The older woman followed her into the bright, sunny den, still scolding. "Leaving the party like that and causing poor Miss Kristina to worry! Not to mention me!"

"Let's do mention you!" Robyn dropped her purse onto the couch and turned with a militant lift of her chin. "I seem to remember someone pestering me to get out of this house once in a while. I even remember at least one distinctly pious wish that I *would* come in with the morning sun!" She glared at the woman who had practically raised her, a challenge in her stance.

Marty maintained her affronted expression for a full minute, then smiled suddenly, her face assuming its usual cheerful look. "So I did," she chuckled. "And it's about time, too! You've been brooding too long, Miss Robyn. There's a time when grieving has to stop. You're too young to bury yourself with Mr. Brian."

Robyn smiled slightly. "I finally let him go, Marty," she confided quietly. "Last night. Even the guilt is gone."

Marty shook her head. "You should never have felt guilt, anyway! You couldn't have stopped Mr. Brian— that day or any other. He was a reckless man; you knew that when you married him."

Robyn shrugged vaguely. "I knew. But . . . Oh, never mind! If you're through fussing, I'd like to have breakfast. I'm starving!"

Her housekeeper and general mother-hen opened her mouth to comment, then apparently thought better of it. Muttering to herself, Marty headed for the kitchen.

Two hours later, refreshed by a shower and breakfast, Robyn lounged by her pool in a brief bikini and blinked like a contented cat at the shimmering blue water. Her thoughts turned to the night before, and she wondered dimly if Shane would be disappointed to wake and find her gone. Probably not. From the look of him, he could certainly have any woman he wanted—and he probably had! One more or less wouldn't matter to him.

Oddly enough, that thought hurt.

"Robyn!"

She turned her head, staring at her cousin who was approaching with a strange look on her face. Robyn felt a flicker of amusement at that look, wondering if Kris would scold her or commend her.

"I nearly died!" Kris exclaimed, her long, graceful body collapsing onto the twin lounge beside Robyn's. "For you to just leave like that—and with Shane Justice, of all people!"

Something tapped at the back of Robyn's mind when she heard his last name, but she ignored it. "Something special about Shane Justice?" she inquired, putting on her sunglasses to hide the intense curiosity she felt. "What . . . is he married?" Sudden dread gripped her even as she haltingly voiced the thought.

"Not that I know of." Kris waved a hand in a vague, bewildered gesture. "But, Robyn—*Shane Justice!*"

Robyn pulled the sunglasses down her nose and peered at her cousin over the top of them. "So?" she questioned blankly.

"You really don't know, do you?" Kris took a deep breath, then said carefully, "Robyn . . . Shane Justice races. Stock cars. Like Brian did."

CHAPTER
Two

FOR AN ETERNAL MOMENT, Robyn continued to stare blankly at her cousin. Then she laughed, a strained laugh, just a whisper away from hysteria. "Isn't that ironic," she said very quietly, a statement rather than a question.

"You really didn't know." It wasn't a question either.

"Do you think I would have left with him if I had?" Robyn tossed the sunglasses onto a table between the lounges. "I swore—*swore*—after Brian was killed that I'd never have anything to do with a man who raced! I must have built-in radar where they're concerned," she went on bitterly. "I'll bet he was the only man there who raced, so of course I had to pick him to—"

"To?" Kris prompted when her cousin broke off abruptly. "Robyn...did you...?"

"I did," Robyn confirmed dully, her earlier con-

15

tentment vanishing as though it had never been. "There was just something about him. I guess he reminded me of Brian, and I thought . . . oh, hell, I don't know what I thought! Nothing intelligent, obviously."

Kris smiled suddenly, her blue eyes showing an unexpected flash of humor. "Oh, I don't know about that! You're certainly looking better than you did this time yesterday. It was just an . . . unusual thing for you to do. Going off with a virtual stranger, I mean. Why, Brian courted you for six months before you were engaged, and I'm willing to bet you didn't sleep with him the whole time!"

Accustomed to her cousin's cheerfully blunt manner, Robyn only smiled wryly. "Maybe I'd had too much to drink," she murmured, trying to rationalize her behavior of the night before.

"Not a chance! You had one drink — a screwdriver, if I remember correctly — and nursed it for nearly an hour. You'll have to come up with a better excuse than that!" She lifted a questioning brow. "Couldn't be love at first sight, could it? It's hardly in character for you to tumble after a single glance!"

"Hardly," Robyn agreed, staring out over the water. "I don't want to fall in love, Kris!" she blurted. "Especially not with a man who races. Life's too short to watch someone you love risk death on a whim."

Kris was silent for a moment, then said dryly, "My feminist friends would kill me for saying this, but you need a man, Robyn. You're the type of woman who'll never be happy living alone. You should have a husband. And kids."

"Maybe I will one day." Determined to change the subject, Robyn spoke in a light voice. "But that husband definitely will *not* be Shane Justice, or anyone like him! He'll be a comfortable, sedate man, with a nine-to-five job and a safe hobby—collecting stamps or something."

Kris gave a crow of laughter. "You'd be bored to tears in a month!" she announced. "Robyn, sweetie, you're just not a comfortable sort of woman!"

"Thanks!" Robyn muttered tartly.

"Well, it's true. You've been in limbo for the past year, ever since Brian was killed. And heaven knows you were nearly out of your mind with terror for him during the year you were married. But your personality is a far cry from 'sedate and comfortable'! You have a temper, for one thing, and you're too damn impulsive for your own good!"

"I am *not* too impulsive!" Robyn defended herself irritably.

"Oh, no?" Kris lifted a mocking brow. "And I suppose last night's decision to leave a party with a man you'd just met, and subsequently spend the night with him, was a carefully thought-out plan?"

A flush crept up into Robyn's cheeks. "I'm twenty-seven years old," she snapped, "and certainly entitled to do whatever I like! If I wanted to spend the night with Shane Justice, then it's my own business."

"Sweetie, I'm not arguing with that." Kris's lovely face brightened suddenly. "In fact, I'm glad you met him! You need the strong, masterful type, and, from what I hear, he's certainly that! But if you're going to see him again—"

"I'm not," Robyn interrupted firmly. She thought again of the night before and shivered slightly. "I'll admit to a certain amount of... attraction, but I'm not about to get involved with a man who's so utterly careless with his own life that he looks for ways to risk it! Shane doesn't even know my last name, so—"

"Maybe not," Kris interjected, a certain satisfaction in her voice, "but he's trying his best to find out."

"What?" Robyn asked uneasily.

Kris grinned and settled back in her lounge. "The phone caught me just as I was leaving my place," she explained cheerfully. "It was Tony—the host of last night's party, remember? Anyway, he sounded very rattled, and he demanded to know my cousin's last name. He complained that I'd introduced you simply as 'my cousin Robyn.' Naturally, I wanted to know *why* he wanted your last name."

"And?" Robyn prompted.

"And," Kris continued obligingly, "he told me that he'd been disturbed at the crack of dawn by a call from Shane Justice, who demanded to know your last name. Tony was so unwise as to ask why Shane hadn't gotten it last night after he left the party with you; he practically got his head bitten off. I gather that Shane can be quite intimidating when he chooses. Anyway, Tony promised to make a few calls and then get back to him. He called me."

"You didn't tell him, did you?" Robyn asked, horrified.

"No, of course not," Kris said soothingly. "I promised to get back to him after I talked to you. I figured that if Shane didn't know your name, you might not want him to know."

"I don't!"

"Then I won't tell Tony. But I have to warn you, sweetie—if Shane is as determined as I think he is, he'll get everything he can out of Tony. And that means *my* name. What am I supposed to say if he comes knocking at my door?"

Robyn chewed on her thumbnail for a moment. "Tell him—tell him that I was just visiting, and that

I've gone home. And make *home* as far away as you can."

Kris giggled. "You know, you're displaying an unholy amount of panic, Robyn. Why? You can always say no if he asks you out! You're not afraid of him, are you?" she asked solicitously.

"Don't be ridiculous; of course I'm not afraid of him." Robyn wasn't about to confess that what she was afraid of were her own feelings. She wanted to see Shane Justice again, and that realization scared her to death. "He'll forget about me soon and race on to whatever's next on the circuit!" she finished bitterly.

"Daytona," Kris murmured soberly. "Tony mentioned that Shane was in Florida for the race. Apparently, he had some business to take care of here in Miami first."

Robyn tried to ignore the information, but her mental calendar automatically registered that the Daytona race was only two weeks away. "There should be no problem; I can avoid him until then," she said calmly.

"I don't know." Her cousin looked at her a little doubtfully. "I've known Tony for five years, and I've never heard him so completely flustered. And it wasn't just a case of morning-after-the-night-before, either. Shane really shook him up. He wants to find you, sweetie—and very badly, I should think. What did you do—put a spell on him?"

Unwillingly, Robyn remembered a deep, husky voice calling her "sweet witch." And "honey," and "sweetheart." Fiercely, she shoved the recollection aside. "He'll forget about me," she repeated stubbornly.

"And what about you?" Kris smiled faintly. "Will you forget about him?"

"He's forgotten," Robyn replied lightly, lying and knowing it. She hopped up from the lounge, determined to change the subject. "I'm going to get dressed and go shopping. Are you game?"

"When have I ever refused shopping?" Kris laughed and rose also, apparently realizing that the subject was closed.

It remained closed for the rest of the weekend. Robyn refused to allow herself to brood about Shane Justice, and she busied herself almost frantically in order to avoid it.

After shopping, she and Kris went horseback riding and then ended up teaching two beginners' classes as a favor to the stable owner, who was a friend of theirs. Although her cousin's students seemed to have grasped the basics, Robyn had to spend over an hour showing her small group the correct way to fall off a horse. One six-year-old in particular won her heart with his fierce determination to master the art, keeping the rest of the pupils in stitches as he gently slid beneath the patient horse's belly again and again.

Sunday was traditionally Robyn's day to help with the housework and washing. Because that didn't keep her as busy as she wanted to be, she also rearranged her bedroom and re-lined the kitchen cabinets.

If Marty thought the unusual burst of energy odd, she said nothing about it. Robyn was too tired on Saturday and Sunday nights to do more than tumble into bed in exhaustion. But she dreamed of eyes of green flame, and a deep, husky voice . . .

Kris called early Monday morning, waking Robyn from her dream-haunted sleep. Robyn rolled over in bed and fumbled for the receiver, mumbling, "What?" when she managed to get it to her ear.

"He came. Last night."

"Who came?" Robyn forced her reluctant eyes open.

"Shane Justice." Kris sounded disgustingly bright-eyed and bushy-tailed. "He offered me everything but an illegal bribe to tell him your last name."

Sitting bolt upright in bed, Robyn awoke with a vengeance. "You didn't tell him?" she wailed.

"Of course not," Kris laughed. "But the man could probably charm a rattlesnake. As it was, I had to keep repeating the multiplication tables in my head in order to maintain control over my own mind."

"Funny," Robyn muttered.

"I thought so." Kris laughed again, cheerfully wished her cousin a good day, and hung up.

Dragging herself from bed, Robyn thoughtfully dressed for work, wondering when Shane would lose patience and give up. Soon, she hoped. She reached into her jewelry box, removed her plain gold wedding band, and slipped it onto her finger. At Marty's insistence she'd finally stopped wearing it to social events, but she was grateful for its repressive effect on her store's male customers.

Moments later, she was driving her small economy car toward the city, wryly remembering Marty's stern command to eat something filling for lunch. She hadn't had much of an appetite during the past year, but then she'd never really been a big eater. She never, much to Kris's loud envy, gained an ounce.

Arriving at her bookstore, she parked her car and went inside, discovering that her assistant, Janie, had already opened up and was busy with several early customers. Placing her purse behind the counter, she began her own work, putting everything else out of her mind.

The morning was hectic, and it was well after noon when things finally quieted down. Glancing sympathetically at her flushed and weary-looking assistant, Robyn grinned. "Okay, Janie, go ahead to lunch. But don't go too far; if I scream hysterically, you have to be near enough to come running!"

"What is it with today?" Janie demanded, leaning against the counter for a moment to recoup her strength. "Is there a blizzard forecast, or what? I've never seen so many people desperately in need of something to read!"

"Beats me, but don't knock it. And get going, before I change my mind and—" Her blonde assistant snatched up her purse and made a mad dash for the door, in so much of a hurry that she nearly collided with the tall red-haired man who was just then coming in.

Holding several books in her arms, Robyn started toward the new customer, feeling a fleeting sense of where-have-I-seen-you-before. "Good afternoon," she said pleasantly. "May I help you?"

His light blue eyes held a peculiar expression as they swept from the smooth coronet of raven hair braided atop her head down over her entire figure, clothed in a casual sundress.

Irritated, Robyn repeated a bit dryly, "May I help you?"

"Um, I'm looking for a book," he announced.

Robyn glanced around at her large store, filled wall-to-wall and floor-to-ceiling with books, and then looked back at the customer. "Well, you've come to the right place," she said, and she watched the tips of his ears redden.

"A book about, uh, about witchcraft!" he elaborated almost defiantly.

Choking back a giggle, Robyn pointed toward a corner of the store. "The occult books are in that section." Odd, she thought, he didn't look the type to be interested in the occult. Well, you never knew these days.

The customer wandered toward the section she'd indicated, and Robyn went back to work, sensing his eyes on her occasionally but ignoring him. He came over to the desk a few minutes later and placed a book on the wooden surface. Scanning the title as she picked up the volume, Robyn shot a faintly amused glance at the man.

"Do you participate in seances?" she asked politely.

He started visibly, confirming her suspicion that he'd simply selected a book at random. "Oh, uh, a friend of mine is. The book's a gift," he explained rather lamely.

Still amused, Robyn rang up the purchase and gave him his change and the book. "Hope your friend enjoys the book."

"I'm sure she will. Thank you, Miss—?" He lifted an eyebrow inquiringly.

"Lee," Robyn supplied calmly, pointedly placing her left hand on the countertop. "Robyn Lee."

His eyes dropped to her hand and widened in surprise. Without another word, he turned on his heel and left the store.

Robyn wondered about his abrupt departure but shrugged it off. When Janie returned, Robyn took a break herself, ducking around the corner to a small Italian restaurant she favored. After a quiet lunch, she returned to find the store fairly calm, so she went into the back room to review the account books.

Janie poked her head in a few minutes later. "Robyn, someone to see you."

Robyn look up, frowning. "Who is it?"

"Never seen him before." Janie grinned. "But if I weren't married . . . !"

Robyn rose from her small desk, groaning, "It's probably a salesman. They're always good-looking.

And that radio station's been pestering me to advertise."

"Well, this guy could sell rocks!" Janie grinned again and headed back into the store.

Sighing, Robyn stepped out of the office and looked toward the front counter. And froze. Of all the thoughts tumbling through her head right then, the only clear one was a panicked, *How did he find me?*

Shane spotted her immediately and began crossing the room toward her. That he was upset was obvious; there was a curious tautness about his lean body, and his face was masklike in its total lack of expression. He halted barely an arm's reach away from her and stood there, staring. She thought she saw relief shine briefly in the emerald eyes—relief and something else, something she couldn't read—but the fleeting expression was quickly gone, leaving only the reflective glow of cut emeralds.

"Hello, Robyn," he greeted quietly.

She felt again that instant attraction, the magnetic pull stronger than anything she had ever known. The sensation frightened her; it was too intense to be real. "H–hello, Shane," she got out weakly.

"You left without saying good-bye."

Robyn gazed up at him uncertainly, puzzled by his voice. He almost sounded as if he were in pain. Nervously clasping her fingers together in front of her, she murmured, "I thought it would be best."

"Why?"

The one word was stark, oddly raw. She had the sudden, insane impression that he was struggling against reaching out and touching her. The impression was so unreasonably strong that she took an instinctive step backward, blinking in bewilderment. Almost immediately, though, she took a firm grip on her imagination.

"Because..." Her voice trailed away as she tried to come up with a logical reason for leaving him without a word. The truth? That she didn't believe in magic, or in anything that was too perfect to be real? That fairy tales happened in fiction but not in fact?

"Dammit, why didn't you tell me?" he rasped suddenly, barely louder than a whisper. "I would have understood, Robyn. People make mistakes. You aren't the type to hop into bed with a stranger just because your marriage went sour; I would have known that. You didn't have to creep away as if you were ashamed of what happened between us! It was special—"

"It wasn't real!" she blurted out suddenly, looking down at the gleaming gold band on her left hand.

Surprisingly, Shane seemed to understand at least a part of what she meant. "It *was* like a dream," he agreed huskily, a faintly twisted smile softening the tautness of his face as she looked up at him. "And we both felt that. But it was right, Robyn, and you know that as well as I do." He hesitated, then began slowly, "Your husband—"

"Is dead," she interrupted, unable to allow him to go on thinking she had broken her marriage vows. "I'm a widow."

"Then..." He stepped toward her quickly, unhidden eagerness leaping into his eyes.

Startled, she said hurriedly, "But I don't want to get involved with you, Shane!" She watched the flame in his eyes die and a baffled expression replace it.

"Why not?" he asked very quietly.

Robyn bit her lip and again sought reasons. Very conscious of customers moving about in the store, and unwilling to go into a long explanation of her fear of racing, she avoided the subject entirely. "Just let it end, Shane, please," she murmured.

"After a night of heaven? I'm a lot of things, honey,

but a fool isn't one of them." His voice was steady.

Desperately, she tried to explain a situation that made no sense, even to herself. "It wasn't *me;* don't you understand? Something happened and—and I don't know what it was! I'm not used to drinking; maybe that was it."

"No." His voice remained steady, the emerald eyes searching her face intently. "You weren't drunk. Robyn, what does it matter *why* it happened? We looked at each other and—"

"It matters!" she cut him off abruptly, afraid of what he might have said. "I've never done anything like that before."

"You don't have to tell me that," he said softly.

"You can't know," she managed unsteadily.

"Can't I?" He smiled slowly, something she didn't understand flaring in his eyes.

For a moment, she felt an almost overpowering impulse to give herself to the magic and let it take her where it would, as it had on Friday night. But she mastered the reckless desire, firmly reminding herself of Shane's racing.

"I don't want to get involved with you," she said flatly.

His smile faded. With obviously forced lightness, he asked, "Is it my breath, or what?"

"Don't be ridiculous." To her astonishment, Robyn found herself choking back a laugh.

"That's better." Clearly approving of the airier atmosphere, he smiled again. "If it isn't my breath," he went on solemnly, "it must be something worse. You don't like the way I dress?"

Beginning to enjoy the exchange, despite the inner voice warning her that every passing moment was involving her more and more with this man, she eyed him consideringly. "You look very nice," she said politely after looking over his slacks and sport shirt.

"Thank you." He inclined his head gravely. "Let's see . . . Green eyes bother you? I'm told mine are a bit startling."

"To say the least," she murmured, thinking of the curious vividness of his eyes. "No, green eyes don't bother me."

"Not that either, huh? Well . . . You don't like my hair?"

"It's a bit shaggy," she pointed out.

"I'll get it cut," he promptly offered.

An uncomfortably clear vision of herself twining her fingers in that dark, slightly shaggy hair flashed through her mind. "No," she muttered. "No, don't get it cut."

"Whatever the lady wants."

The vision had drained her amusement. "What the lady wants," she said quietly, "is for you to leave her alone."

He reached out suddenly, one hand cupping her cheek warmly, and she was surprised to feel a faint tremor in his fingers.

"I can't do that." The words were carefully spaced, emphasized with soft fierceness. "I can't walk away from you, Robyn. And I won't give up what we found together the other night. I don't know what you're afraid of, but I'm not going to give you up. I'll just go on asking until I find out what's wrong."

Bemused by the tingling shock of his touch as well as by his words, Robyn stared up at him for a long moment. She wasn't quite sure how to deal with this man. His determination to go on seeing her in the face of her refusal seemed unshaken. He hadn't even been angry at finding out—how had he found out?—

that she was married; he had seemed more hurt because she hadn't told him herself. How strange. In Shane's place, Brian would have been furious.

She swallowed hard. "This is the twentieth century, Shane. I don't have to see anyone I don't want to see."

"Then tell me that." His voice was still softly insistent. "Tell me that you never want to see me again. Truthfully."

Robyn dropped her gaze. "I—"

"Look at me!" His fingers tightened slightly against her skin. "Look me in the eye, Robyn. I have to know that you're telling me the truth."

"You're not being fair," she accused him unsteadily, looking up once more. His emerald eyes allowed her no escape, holding her own with an intensity that bewildered her. "Shane, please . . ."

He swore softly beneath his breath and glanced around at the busy store. "This is no place for us to talk. What time does the store close, Robyn?"

"Shane—"

"What time?" He shook his head slowly as he met the appeal in her eyes. "I can't let it end like this, honey. I can't."

Robyn felt her resolve weakening, something in the emerald eyes draining her willpower. "Five," she murmured at last. "The store closes at five."

"I'll pick you up out front," he said.

Robyn again thought she saw relief flicker in his eyes, but she simply nodded weakly. Her nerve endings tingled again as he softly brushed his fingers against her cheek. Then he was striding from the store.

She stared after him for an eternal moment. Catching Janie's questioning glance, she smiled—reassuringly, she hoped. Automatically looking around to make sure she wasn't needed at the moment, she turned and hurried back to her tiny office.

Sitting behind her desk, she watched her hands shake for a good ten minutes.

"Idiot," she muttered, addressing the boxes of books stacked all around her. "Damned fool. He races. *Races.* You can't take that again. You know you can't."

Thoughts of racing inevitably brought Brian to mind, and she wondered again at Shane's lack of temper. He hadn't raised his voice once, she remembered. A man worth knowing...

"No," she told the boxes again. "You just miss Brian, that's all."

In spite of herself, she remembered Friday night. She had never felt such grinding need with Brian. She had never felt such a fierce desire, a primitive yearning, to join herself to him body and soul. He had never roused in her the feelings she remembered so clearly from her magical night with Shane.

A little desperately, Robyn pushed the thoughts away. She had imagined the depths of those feelings, she told herself firmly. It was only because she'd been so long without Brian.

It was nothing more than that. Never mind the strange shock of recognition she'd felt in that first moment. Never mind the staggering bolt of electricity arcing between green eyes and gold across a crowded room. Never mind the dazed, churning thoughts that had filled her mind, thoughts of fate and destiny and sheer luck. Never mind the sense of utter belonging she'd felt in his arms...

At five o'clock, determinedly hiding her nervousness, she waved good-bye to Janie and locked up the store, realizing even before she looked that Shane was standing behind her. Dropping her keys into her purse, she turned slowly and stared up at him.

"Ready?" he asked, taking her arm and beginning to lead her toward the black Porsche parked by the curb.

"Would it matter if I said no?" she muttered.

"Not a bit," he told her cheerfully, guiding her around to the passenger side of the gleaming car and opening the door for her.

Robyn sighed as she took her place inside and watched him close her door and walk around the car again. His first words when he got into the car caught her off guard.

"How long have you been a widow?"

She found her fingers twining together nervously in her lap. "A little more than a year."

"And how long have you owned that store?"

"What is this—twenty questions?"

"If you like."

She watched his profile as he started the car and pulled out into the stream of rush-hour traffic. "I've owned the store for about three months," she answered finally.

"Did you work while your husband was alive?"

"No," she replied stiffly. She didn't know why, but she felt very uneasy talking to Shane about her marriage.

He shot a glance at her, and his barrage of questions ceased. She was relieved when he began speaking in a casual, friendly tone. "My family owns a wine business in California. My parents began it more than thirty years ago, and Mother still keeps a firm hand on the reins." He chuckled softly. "She keeps threatening to retire and shove everything onto my shoulders, but I don't think it's very likely. Especially since she violently disapproves of my 'hobby'."

Her relief evaporated. "Your hobby?" she asked politely, already knowing the answer.

"I race stock cars."

"Oh." For the life of her, she couldn't think of anything else to say. Not wanting him to know about her reluctant involvement in racing, she thought it best to betray no knowledge of the sport. He had probably met Brian, and would certainly recognize her married name if she revealed it.

"That's one of the reasons I'm in Florida," he continued cheerfully. "I intend to qualify for Daytona."

Robyn had to change the subject; she couldn't bear to think about racing, let alone talk about it. "Where are we going?" she asked.

He glanced at her again and replied softly, "I know a quiet restaurant nearby. It's a little early for dinner, but we need somewhere to talk. Somewhere public, I think." He seemed to hesitate, then added with outrageous calm, "With other people around, I might—possibly—be able to keep my hands off you."

She felt a flush coat her cheeks in scarlet, and her mind spun crazily. Good Lord, but he didn't pull his punches! Never in her life had she met a man like him. Desire, she had been taught, was a very private thing. Abruptly, she remembered her own behavior of Friday night, and her flush deepened. Well, maybe he had good reason to speak so bluntly!

He was laughing softly. "After Friday night, you surely can't doubt that I want you?" That peculiar huskiness was suddenly back in his voice, turning the soft question into a caress.

Robyn shifted uneasily on the narrow bucket seat. "I don't want to get involved with you, Shane," she repeated for what felt like the hundredth time.

"Too late now," he responded lightly.

She stared at him, her mind working with the grinding slowness of dry gears. No, it wasn't too late. There was only one reasonable explanation for what had happened on Friday night. The magic, the dreamlike feeling... She had pretended Shane was Brian.

It was the only thing that made sense. Hadn't she failed to ask his name because that would have ruined her dream? Hadn't she wished his green eyes blue?

Almost blindly, she watched Shane pull the powerful little car into a parking place in front of an elegant-looking restaurant.

No, it wasn't too late. All she had to do was tell Shane the truth. He had been a stand-in for a ghost. That should quite effectively destroy his hopes for a relationship between them. She wouldn't have to live in fear again...

Shane switched off the ignition, smiled suddenly, and reached out to cup her cheek in one large, warm hand. "Why so worrried?" he asked softly. "It can't be as bad as that, surely!"

Robyn felt his thumb move lightly across her lips, and she fought back a shiver as her body responded wildly to the tiny caress. *It shouldn't be this way!* a panicked voice inside her head screamed.

Before she could begin to think clearly, he groaned deep in his chest and abruptly leaned across the console, his green eyes gleaming like gems.

"Just let me kiss you," he breathed.

Robyn made no effort to stop him, although the little voice continued to scream warnings. His lips touched hers gently, and a sigh seemed to rise from deep inside her.

With his familiar lion's growl, Shane deepened the kiss, his hand sliding down to encircle her throat. His tongue explored her mouth, taking full advantage of her lack of resistance. His free hand moved suddenly, slipping around her waist and then sliding up to draw her upper body firmly against his across the console.

Robyn lost herself in the warm, drugging feel of his embrace, telling herself silently that there was no danger here—not in a car parked at a restaurant. But she knew there was danger. The problem was that the danger was inside her. She couldn't seem to fight the flood of sensations elicited by his touch.

Her hand lifted of its own volition to touch his lean cheek, needing the fleeting contact for some reason her mind didn't begin to understand.

With an obvious effort, he tore his lips from hers at last, muttering a violent, "*Damn* sports cars!" He drew slowly away from her, the tautness of his body betraying an impatient restlessness. "Next time I'll drive something without a gear console!"

Coming abruptly to her senses, Robyn stared at him with a surge of panic. What was wrong with her? With every moment that passed, she was becoming more drawn into this man, and it would only hurt more when...

"Don't worry, little witch." He was laughing. "We'll talk first. But you're going to have a hard time keeping me at bay!"

Feeling a sudden, aching sadness mixed with weary relief, she watched him slide out of the car and come around to open her door. She would not, she knew, have to keep him at bay. Once he found out why she'd gone with him that night, he would want to have nothing more to do with her.

He would quite probably hate her.

He helped her from the car, and they silently entered the restaurant. The place was dim and shadowy and nearly deserted at that time of day. They were led to a corner table, and Shane looked inquiringly at Robyn when a waiter approached.

"A drink for now? We can order later."

She nodded and murmured, "White wine," then watched as Shane relayed their order to the waiter.

As the waiter left, Shane reached across the table to cover her hands with one of his. His smile suddenly faded. He lifted her left hand, frowning. "Take it off," he ordered.

"What?" She stared at him blankly, not understanding.

"When you're with me, you won't wear another man's ring," he told her tautly. "Take it off, Robyn . . . please."

She hesitated for a moment, then removed the ring and placed it in her purse. She knew the meek obedience was uncharacteristic, but she didn't feel up to making a stand on the subject of her ring—especially as she was already dreading the anger her confession would certainly provoke.

Still holding her left hand with his right, Shane leaned back in his chair and smiled. "That ring threw poor Eric for a loop," he murmured almost to himself.

"Eric?"

He nodded. "Eric. A friend of mine. He knew that I was tearing Miami apart to find a raven-haired, golden-eyed witch named Robyn, he just happened to stumble into your bookstore, and you were wearing a wedding ring. He didn't know whether to call me or just to hope I never found you."

"The man with red hair," she murmured, suddenly realizing why the customer had looked so familiar. "He was with you at the party." She flushed as his comment about tearing apart Miami sunk in, and dropped her gaze to the cream-colored tablecloth.

The waiter approached with their wine, and Robyn tried to pull her hand away from Shane's. She was suddenly aware that they must look like new lovers, and the image disturbed her.

But he wouldn't release her hand, holding it firmly as he smiled absently at the waiter. One of his fingers trailed across her palm in a strangely intimate little caress, and Robyn shivered, feeling nerves all through her body prickle to awareness.

After the waiter had deposited their glasses and left, Shane turned his full attention back to her, his green eyes warming almost as though the sight of her delighted him. "You look very beautiful today," he said softly. "Cool and calm—except for the slight trace of panic in your eyes."

Hastily, Robyn lifted her glass and took a sip of wine. She didn't want him to talk like that, flattering though it was. "Don't you want to know why I don't want to get involved with you?" she asked uneasily.

"Later," he answered easily. "You and I are going to have dinner and talk, get to know each other. Then we'll go back to my place, or yours, if you prefer. That'll be soon enough for explanations."

Somewhat to her surprise, Robyn found herself relaxing as the time passed. Shane, she found, was an interesting conversationalist, and he possessed a sinful amount of charm. He never once broached the subject of her marriage, but his casual questions covered practically every other phase of her life.

Astonished, she found herself telling him about her rootless childhood: about her mother, who'd died when Robyn was three; about her career-army father, whom she'd followed from base to base; and about Marty, who had raised her. Shane told her bits and pieces of his childhood in turn, confessing a love for animals and a powerful affection for his strong-willed mother.

It was a peculiar interlude, Robyn realized. Having leaped headfirst into the most intimate of relationships, they were now backtracking slowly, almost feeling their way.

She wanted to keep the conversation away from racing, but since that was a large part of Shane's life, the subject inevitably came up.

"My family wants me to settle down," he was saying now, casually. "I'm usually on the road from January through September, following the circuit."

"And the rest of the time?" she asked, toying with her wine glass.

"Wine." He smiled slowly at her puzzled expression. "The vineyards," he clarified. "Of course, I take care of a lot of the business even when I'm on the road. But I really get into the thick of things when I'm back home."

"Do you enjoy the wine business?" she asked curiously.

"Sure. I've grown up in it. I helped harvest the grapes when I was just a kid. As a matter of fact, my father used to say that I was always underfoot—and making a nuisance of myself."

Robyn tried to picture an eager, black-haired little boy with bright green eyes, but the grown man across the table from her kept getting in the way. Her awareness of him was so powerful it felt almost like a fixation.

And that was scary. It didn't fit in with her neat little explanation for Friday night. But if Shane hadn't been just a reminder of Brian, then why had she . . . ?

Robyn thrust the half-formed question from her mind. Of course he had been; there was no other possible explanation.

She would tell Shane the truth. He would be angry. Angry and probably disgusted. He would leave her life as abruptly as he had entered it. And he would leave hating her.

But it had to be that way. Involvement with him

would only plunge her back into the strangling web of worry and terror that her marriage to Brian had woven around her. She wouldn't let that happen; her confession would drive him away from her.

Now . . . before it was too late.

CHAPTER
Three

HOURS LATER, SHANE pulled the Porsche to a stop in the driveway of Robyn's home. She had chosen her own place rather than his hotel mainly because she had a feeling that she just might need moral support once Shane knew the truth. At least here she had Marty, although, judging by the darkened house, Marty was already in bed.

It was late. They had stayed in the restaurant for hours, then simply driven around Miami, still talking. Weary with pondering her emotions, Robyn had allowed herself—or, rather, forced herself—to think of the meeting as just another date, one that would be ending any time now.

"Nice place." Shane got out of the car and came around to open her door. "A little big, though."

Robyn waited until they were standing beneath the

front porch light before responding to his comment, and when she did speak it was in a very deliberate tone. "Brian bought it shortly after we were married. We both wanted a large family." She sensed him tensing beside her, but she continued to pay careful attention to locating the keys in her purse.

Once they were found, she unlocked the door and silently moved ahead of him into the house, leading the way to the den, where a lamp burned. She turned on another lamp and dropped her purse into a chair, trying to fight the cravenness inside her that wanted to avoid this confrontation at all costs.

"Robyn—"

"There's the bar," she said quickly, pointing to one corner of the large room. "Help yourself."

Shane stared at her for a moment, obviously puzzled by her nervousness, then strode across the room and splashed some brandy into a snifter. He looked over his shoulder at her. "What will you have?"

"Nothing." Robyn had never in her life wanted a drink as badly as she did right then, but she knew Dutch courage wouldn't help her. She sank down onto the couch and watched as he came over to lower his weight beside her. When he put his arm around her, she straightened tensely.

"Robyn . . ." There was a curiously bleak tone to his voice. "Honey, don't pull away from me."

She glanced at him, then rose to her feet, turning to face him and feeling a little less intimidated because he was still seated. Her mind kept repeating *Get it over with* as though it were a litany.

Steadily, she said, "Friday night was a mistake, Shane. What you think is between us—it isn't real."

He sipped his brandy slowly, watching her through hooded green eyes. "It felt real enough to me," he objected quietly.

"That's because you don't know why—why I left with you. Why it all happened."

"Then tell me." He continued to watch her steadily. "Why did it all happen?"

Almost inaudibly, she whispered, "You reminded me of—of Brian."

For a long moment, she thought he hadn't heard her, or hadn't understood. Then, with unnatural care, he reached out to set his glass on an end table, his eyes never leaving her face. And suddenly those emerald eyes were the only splash of color in his whitened face.

"What?" His voice was quiet, as unnaturally calm as his movements of a moment before.

A flashing memory of some of Brian's rages made Robyn take an instinctive step backward, but even as she did so she realized that Shane wasn't angry. Instead, he seemed stunned. Would the rage come later?

"You . . . you reminded me of my husband, and I wanted to . . . spend one last night with him. It was a dream! It wasn't real!" she defended herself shakily.

Shane abruptly rose to his feet, as though he couldn't be still any longer, as though he desperately needed to move. "You pretended I was your dead husband?" he asked in a curiously dazed voice.

"I'm sorry," she whispered, wanting suddenly to unsay the words, to wipe away the horrible stricken look on his face.

"Sorry," he repeated dully. "You're sorry." He turned away from her and walked jerkily to the window, standing with his back to her and staring out the window into darkness. "Too perfect to be real," he murmured, as if to himself.

Robyn wrapped her arms around herself, trying in vain to ward off the chill invading her. She didn't know how to cope with this; the intensity of his emotions unnerved her. Anger she had been prepared for, but this strange, quiet agony was totally unexpected. It was somehow more upsetting than rage would have been.

"You should have just let it end, Shane," she said huskily. "You shouldn't have made me tell you." He swung around abruptly and came toward her, and she involuntarily shrank back.

But the large hands that grasped her shoulders were as gentle as though they held a fragile, frightened bird. Though the green eyes were fierce, there was no anger in them. Only disbelief.

"Tell me you lied, Robyn," he said hoarsely, the words a plea rather than a command. "Tell me there was no ghost in my bed that night!"

She shook her head silently, not trusting herself to speak.

"I don't believe you," he grated softly. "No, I don't believe you." His head swooped suddenly, taking her completely by surprise.

As his lips captured hers, his hands sliding down her back to pull her slender body almost roughly against the hardness of his, Robyn found herself totally unable to struggle. She told herself vaguely that it was the abruptness of his attack, the strength of his embrace, that had drained her resistance.

Except that it wasn't an attack.

His lips moved on hers with gentle, insidious persuasion, pleading for rather than demanding a response. Of their own volition Robyn's arms slid around his neck, her lips parting instinctively beneath his. She felt the now familiar flood of wild emotion sweep her body, and she gave herself up totally to the joy of the feelings he aroused in her.

He slid the zipper of her strapless sundress down, and the colorful material fell in a heap around her feet. The cool air on her skin seemed to intensify the raging sensations in her body, bringing a vivid, almost painful awareness to her fogged senses.

She felt his tongue moving in a possessive invasion of her mouth, and she found herself mindlessly responding, her own tongue joining his in a passionate duel. A sudden feeling of vertigo told her that he had lifted her into his arms, and then she felt the softness of the plush couch beneath her back.

Tearing his lips from hers, Shane pressed hot kisses down her throat to the pulse beating madly in the hollow of her shoulder. Robyn bit her lip with a soft moan as he expertly unfastened the front clasp of her strapless bra and smoothed the lacy material aside.

"Tell me you lied," he whispered raggedly, sensually abrasive fingers tracing the curve of her full breast, thumb and forefinger tugging gently at the hardening nipple. "Dammit, tell me you lied!"

His harsh, cracked voice and the demand he made vibrated against her flesh, somehow making its way through the veils of need and desire. Realizing that her lips had parted to tell him just what he wanted to hear, she felt panic sweep over her.

"No," she moaned desperately, her arms falling away from him as she tried to gain control over her scattered senses.

"You lied," he grated roughly, his fingers locking in her hair as he raised his head and stared down at her. "You lied to me, didn't you?"

Robyn saw something terrible happening in his eyes, on his face. She had never before seen such sheer primitive emotion in a man, such naked hunger, and it awed her as rage never could have.

"No," she repeated in a whisper, trying to shrink away from him. "I told you the truth."

He stared down at her, breathing raspily, for a long

moment. Then, as though it were torture for him, he pulled himself away from her to sit on the edge of the couch. "You're afraid of me," he muttered in obvious disbelief, shock adding to the whirlpool of emotion in his eyes. "My God, you're afraid of me!"

Robyn's fear drained away as she realized finally, completely, that Shane wouldn't hurt her. As obviously upset as he was—had been, from the moment of her confession—he was in complete control of whatever disturbing emotions he felt. But before she could say anything, he had risen to his feet, still gazing down at her.

"Dammit to hell, Robyn—" He broke off abruptly and strode to the door, looking back over his shoulder only once, his face taut and masklike. And then he was gone.

Automatically, Robyn fastened her bra and dragged herself from the couch to find and put on her dress. Listening to the violent roar of the Porsche as it pulled out of her drive, she murmured very softly to the empty room, "Liar."

She had lied to him, told him something no one should ever have to hear—that he had been a stand-in for another man.

She knew then that she hadn't pretended Shane was her husband on Friday night. Not even in the beginning. Even when she had wished his green eyes blue, there had been no ghost between them. She had only been trying to find some reasonable, rational explanation for what had been happening between them—for her own irrational, uncharacteristic behavior. And she'd latched on to pretending that a stranger was her husband. It was not an impossible fantasy. Contemptible, perhaps—certainly pathetic. But not impossible.

Love at first sight was impossible. Not reasonable

or rational. Not *real*. A dream. Two people finding one another by chance, by fate, sharing a dream.

But the dream had shattered the moment she'd found out that Shane Justice raced. Like Brian had.

Feeling a misery such as she had never known, Robyn silently turned off the lamps and made her way from the den, heading for the wing of the house that contained its five spacious bedrooms. The hall light came on as she was crossing the foyer, and Marty came forward, wearing a battered robe over her nightgown.

"Robyn?" Dispensing with the half-teasing formality she normally assumed, the older woman sounded concerned. "Are you all right? I thought I heard—" She broke off abruptly as Robyn came fully into the light.

"I'm fine," Robyn answered quietly. Noticing Marty's stare, she put up a hand to find that her cheeks were wet. Odd, she hadn't even realized she was crying.

In a strange tone, Marty said, "I haven't seen you cry since you were a little girl. Not even when your father died. Not even when Brian was killed. What's happened, Robyn?"

Not sure herself, Robyn could only shrug wearily.

Marty glanced toward the front door. "I heard a car leave. Was it the man from Friday night, Robyn?" She had wormed the bare facts from Robyn and Kris and, while not condemning Robyn's behavior, she clearly hadn't entirely approved, either.

"Yes." Robyn tried a smile and knew from Marty's expression that it hadn't come off. "He won't be back, though."

"Why not?"

Almost whispering, Robyn replied, "Because I sent him away, Marty. I sent him away hating me."

Despite the fact that Marty knew who—and what—Shane Justice was, and that she probably had a good idea why Robyn had "sent him away," she asked the question anyway. In the quiet, motherly tone that had pulled Robyn through both childhood disasters and adult tragedies, she urged, "Why, honey?"

Robyn felt fresh tears spill from her eyes; it was beyond her ability to halt them. "Because I'm a coward," she said starkly.

Robyn went to work the next morning at her normal time, and, between the heavier-than-usual makeup and her rigid control, neither Janie nor any of the customers noticed anything out of the ordinary.

Her night had been tormented and sleepless, filled with painful thoughts on the ironies of love. What punishing Fate had decreed that she was to fall in love with two men in her life—both of them obsessed with a dangerous sport that terrified her?

Kris had been right in her speculation, and Robyn no longer fought the knowledge that she had fallen in love with Shane that first night. With that first glance, in fact.

She should have realized from the very beginning. Her own response to Shane should have told her the truth. Sex and love had always been inextricably tied together in her mind. If she didn't feel love, she didn't make love . . . and she had made love with Shane.

It had taken months for her to be certain of her love for Brian. And even then she had hesitated, torn by her fear of his racing. But her feelings for Shane had overpowered hesitation. She had loved him, and, loving him, had wanted only to be with him.

But Shane raced, and it would have torn her apart to watch him risk his life over and over again.

With Brian, she had been able to stand it for nearly

a year. But, although it shocked her to admit it even silently, her love for her husband had been tame compared to the wild, desperate yearning of her love for Shane. What would it have done to her to love him with her entire being—perhaps even to be loved in return—and then lose him?

It would kill her, her heart answered.

So she had driven him away. Before she could commit herself to that love. Before she could—

"Excuse me?"

Robyn looked up hastily, the familiar surroundings of her store—and the red-haired, blue-eyed man staring at her across the desk—coming into focus. Shane's friend. Eric?

"Excuse me, Mrs. Lee—"

"Ms.," she corrected calmly, not wanting to explain that Lee was her maiden name.

"Ms. Lee." He looked a bit uncertain. "I'm looking for Shane. I was wondering if you might know where he is."

Robyn frowned at him, pushing her disturbed thoughts away. "No. Why would I know?"

"He was with you last night..."

She stiffened and then relaxed suddenly, telling herself wryly that she was going to explode one day if she kept letting tension get to her this way. "He left my place sometime around midnight," she told Shane's friend quietly. "I haven't seen him since."

It was Eric's turn to frown. "He hasn't been back to his hotel. It isn't like him to just disappear—"

"I told you years ago not to worry about me, friend."

It was Shane, and Robyn didn't know whether to kiss him or throw a book at him. She did neither. What she did do was stare at him with wide eyes.

Eric, too, turned to stare at his friend, one rusty

eyebrow rising. "Well, you're certainly looking chipper," he grumbled in mock disgust.

Not having given Robyn a single direct look, Shane responded calmly. "Why shouldn't I? I had a shave and a shower—at the hotel, by the way. The desk clerk told me I'd just missed you."

Robyn searched his appearance guardedly, noting the still-damp hair, the casual slacks, and the fresh pullover knit shirt. He didn't look as if *his* night had been filled with violent emotions, but something in his eyes told Robyn that he had slept no better than she. Why was he here?

Eric was speaking in a faintly harassed tone. "Well, next time, how about giving me notice if you plan to stay out all night? I got a call late last night from Sonny. He said the truck broke down in some little town in Georgia, and it'll take a couple of days to find the parts they need. The car won't be in Daytona until the weekend."

Shane frowned and then shrugged. "Soon enough. That'll give me a week before the trials. How about the pit crew?"

"On their way." Eric grinned. "Sonny had to bail three of them out of jail in South Carolina. A brawl in a bar, I think he said."

Shane laughed, but before he could respond, Robyn, tired of being virtually ignored, broke in irritably, "If you gentlemen wouldn't mind very much, I'd appreciate it if you took your business somewhere else. This is a bookstore, not a racetrack!"

As if he hadn't heard her, Shane said calmly, "Robyn, this is the friend I was telling you about. You two haven't been properly introduced. Robyn Lee—Eric Michaels."

"Ms. Lee." Eric was smiling in a friendly manner.

Inwardly sighing, she murmured, "Robyn—
please." She leaned an elbow on the high counter and
propped her chin in her hand, one part of her ruefully
appreciative of the moment. Each time she'd thought
herself free of Shane's presence, he'd somehow reap-
peared. Worse than a boomerang, she silently groused,
wishing that her eyes would quit sneaking glances at
his face.

Incredibly, her sense of humor had reasserted itself, and she didn't bother to wonder why. She was
tired of brooding, tired of worrying about things that
hadn't happened yet. One day at a time—that was
the ticket. For now, she was just glad that Shane had
come back—for whatever reason.

"Robyn it is, then." His smile turning into a cheerful grin, Eric added conversationally, "You know, I
meant to tell you yesterday how glad I am that Shane
met you. I've been warning him for years that one
day he'd join the human race and take his fall just
like the rest of us poor mortals. Trouble was, he never
believed me. I'm sure he does now, though."

"That's enough, Eric," Shane said mildly.

Robyn looked from one to the other of them, more
than a little puzzled. "Clue me in?" she requested
politely.

"Eric never makes sense," Shane told her easily,
casting a sidelong glance at his friend.

As if that look had been a signal, Eric immediately
began making getting-ready-to-leave noises. "Yes.
Well. It was nice seeing you again, Robyn. I, uh, I'm
having a little party at my place tomorrow night; I'd
like for you to come."

"She'll be there," Shane responded before Robyn
could even open her mouth. "And, if you ask her
nicely, she might even bring her cousin along."

Eric cocked a quizzical brow at his friend. "You

mean the leggy blonde I somehow missed at the party Friday night? The one you said was a knockout?"

"The very same."

With a purely masculine gleam in his blue eyes, Eric smiled charmingly at Robyn. "By all means, bring her along!"

"I'll pass along the invitation," Robyn replied, not committing herself one way or the other. No matter what Shane said.

"Good enough." Eric waved cheerfully at them both and left the store.

Robyn watched him go, avoiding Shane's gaze as long as possible. Tuesday was a slow day for the store; at the moment, the place was empty. Janie had gone to lunch, so they were alone.

She finally looked at Shane as he leaned against the counter, very much aware of their solitude. Trying to think of something casual to say, she murmured, "He's more than a friend, isn't he? He has something to do with your . . . hobby."

Shane nodded, watching her with curious, inscrutable intensity. "He generally takes care of details for me. Deals with the sponsors, makes sure the car and the pit crew are where they're supposed to be. Since I travel so much, Mother saddles me with the family business, and it's a little hectic to take care of both. Eric has a house here in Florida, though. North Miami."

Suddenly determined, Robyn met his gaze squarely. "I didn't expect to see you again."

He shook his head slowly, still watching her intently. "After what happened last night, I'm not surprised."

Robyn made a vague gesture with one hand. "Then why are you here, Shane? Last night—"

"Last night I was upset, and not thinking too clearly," he interrupted flatly. "You threw me a curve,

and it wasn't the easiest thing in the world to accept."
He sighed softly. "I spent most of the night walking
along the beach and thinking. Somewhere around
dawn, I finally realized that there was something off-
center about your explanation."

"Off-center?" Surely he hadn't discovered the truth!

"Yes. You might very well have . . . pretended that
I was your husband on Friday night." His face tight-
ened on the last words, and there was a brief flash of
something uncomfortably grim in his eyes, then he
went on softly. "But you weren't pretending last night.
You knew damn well who was making love to you.
There was no ghost between us. And you wanted me.
Me, Robyn."

Robyn hastily picked up a pencil on the desk and
began toying with it, watching her fingers. "So?"

"So . . . despite whatever you still feel for your husband, you want me. You feel the same desire that I
feel for you."

"Desire isn't exactly uncommon." She forced an
uncaring lightness into her voice. "If you believe movies and television, it's practically epidemic."

"Not the kind we have." He leaned forward slightly,
his green eyes darkening. "I'm thirty-four years old,
Robyn. I've felt desire for a woman. I've felt desire
in a woman. But not like what we have. And I'm not
willing to throw that away."

She watched one of his hands reach out to cover
her restless ones, and she instinctively looked up to
meet his intent gaze. "What are you saying, Shane?"
she whispered, her heart clenching in a sudden com-
bination of pain and hope.

Slowly, as if he were uncertain about how to word
it, Shane answered, "We owe each other something.
We owe each other an opportunity to find out if this

desire we feel is real, if it can grow into something more. Our first night together, you may or may not have thought of me as someone else. Last night, I walked out on you. We haven't given ourselves a chance, Robyn."

She felt the hand covering hers tighten, and she sensed a strange tension in him as he waited for her response. Did it matter so much to him, she wondered dimly. "Are you suggesting an affair?" she asked slowly.

Immediately, he shook his head. "No. The opposite of an affair, Robyn. I'm suggesting a friendship."

"Do you think that's possible, Shane?" she murmured.

"Yes," he responded firmly. "It's possible. We started out all wrong. Instead of first becoming friends, we became lovers . . . for whatever reasons." A hint of grimness crept into his tone and then disappeared as he went on. "We broke all the rules by starting out that way—and probably short-circuited all our instincts as well. What we need is a little time to get to know each other, uncomplicated by a physical relationship."

"And—and if we find that we can't be friends?"

"Then we won't have lost anything, will we?" He sighed, the emerald eyes rueful. "I don't expect it to be easy, Robyn—for me, at least. I expect a lot of sleepless nights and more than one cold shower." Robyn felt herself flush at his bluntness, and his voice was amused when he continued, "But I'm willing to try."

Robyn told herself that she'd be an idiot to agree to anything this man asked of her. She told herself that familiarity would only deepen the emotions that already had the power to make her doubt her own sanity. And then where would she be? But she wasn't very surprised to hear herself agreeing to his suggestion.

"All right, Shane."

His hand tightened almost painfully over hers for a moment and then relaxed. "Terrific. Now, I have a question...friend."

Robyn felt a smile tugging at her lips as she stared into the laughing emerald eyes. "And what's that...friend?"

"Do you think your assistant could run the store for you for a few days?"

"Why?"

"Because, in the interest of getting to know one another, I propose that we spend some time alone together. I have a little trip in mind."

Robyn thought of Daytona and felt her face stiffen. "A trip?" she asked unevenly.

"That's right. Eric has a sailboat he's offered to lend me. I thought we could take a few days and sail down along the keys." He grinned. "Swim, fish, cultivate an indecent tan. What do you think?"

Robyn was so relieved to avoid the possibility of going near a racetrack that for a moment she couldn't say anything. Shane obviously misunderstood her silence.

"Robyn? Will you trust me to keep to our bargain? We'll have separate cabins on the boat."

"It's not that, Shane. It's just..."

"Just what?"

She paused, uncertain how to object. Suddenly laughing, she challenged: "Who's going to do the cooking?"

With a startled chuckle, he responded, "We'll share the galley duty—how's that?"

"Well, all right. But I have to warn you; the only

thing I know about sailboats is to duck when the boom swings across!" She stared at him with mock sternness. "I hope you know more than that, or heaven only knows where we'll end up."

"I know enough to keep us off reefs and sandbars, and to get us there and back in one piece," he said huffily. "It's been a few years, but I've sailed the keys."

Robyn glanced at the door as a customer came in, then looked back at Shane. "Can you afford to take the time? I mean, with the race coming up...?"

"We should be back by Monday, which will give me plenty of time." He smiled at her. "We'll start out early tomorrow morning, okay? I'll check out the boat and stock the galley this afternoon."

"Fine. What time tomorrow?" Robyn was astonished at her easy acceptance.

"I'll pick you up at eight." He waited for her nod and then turned away, only to turn back. "Uh oh, I just remembered something."

"What?"

"Eric will kill me if your cousin doesn't show up at his party tomorrow night!"

Robyn laughed. "Give him Kris's number and tell him to call her tomorrow. Once I describe him, she'll go to the party!"

He lifted an eyebrow. "I'd like to hear that description."

She smiled sweetly. "See you tomorrow... friend."

CHAPTER
Four

"YOU'RE GOING *WHERE?* With *who?*"

"Whom," Robyn corrected in a deliberately off-hand voice, frowning down at the selection of clothing laid out on her bed. She was trying to think of a reasonable answer to the question she knew her cousin was on the point of asking.

Kris made a rude noise and ignored the correction of her bad grammar. "You're really going sailing with Shane Justice?" She looked over at Marty. "Is she crazy?"

"She says not." Marty's voice was as grim as her face. "I'll take leave to doubt that, though."

Her gaze swinging back to Robyn, Kris said carefully, "You're jumping into this—this relationship with Shane awfully quickly, sweetie. Are you sure, you're not—"

"Rushing things?" Robyn looked up at last, a faint smile lifting her lips. "That's what this trip is for—to make sure we . . . get off on the right foot." Her smile faded but didn't entirely disappear. She added quietly, "Brian's dead, Kris. And he wouldn't have wanted me to grieve forever."

Kris made another rude noise. "He wouldn't have grieved this long. For you, I mean." She hesitated when Robyn frowned at her, then went on coolly, "He wasn't a very deep person emotionally, you know. I'm not saying he didn't love you; he loved you as much as he could, being Brian." When Robyn made no response, Kris sighed and ruthlessly returned to the original topic. "Why go with Shane? He races, Robyn, and you can't take that. You know you can't!"

Robyn rolled up a colorful T-shirt and stuffed it into the duffel bag at her feet. "We're going sailing, Kris, not getting married."

Kris sank down onto the opposite side of the bed and gazed at Robyn with transparent concern. "You're getting involved with him, Robyn. You got involved with him that first night. I don't want to see you terrified out of your mind like you were with Brian. It'd kill you this time."

Hearing Kris echo her own earlier thoughts, Robyn absently stuffed a bikini into the bag, then looked across the bed levelly. "Would it? I don't know. But I know one thing, Kris." She included Marty in her level stare. "I can't walk away from Shane just because I'm afraid. And I can't go through life being afraid of things I can't change. If I do, I'll become an emotional cripple."

Kris was frowning now as she stared at her cousin; Marty looked thoughtful, her face unreadable. Robyn continued calmly.

"I may live to regret it, I know. The thought of

going through what I went through with Brian makes
me sick to my stomach. But I won't walk away from
Shane without giving myself a chance." She hesitated,
then finished almost in a whisper, "Love's so rare. I
owe it to myself to see if I can find it again. A stronger
love. A mutual love."

"Something tells me," Kris said very quietly, "that
you've already found it. That's why you're going with
Shane, isn't it?"

Robyn abandoned pretense. "It's another chance,
Kris. And I can't throw that away."

Robyn thought about her own words as she lay in
bed that night, wondering if she were only fooling
herself. She turned restlessly and pounded her pillow
in irritation. It was useless, this soul-searching. Utterly useless. She and Shane would have a nice little
trip, and that would be the end of it. Maybe.

She was still trying to convince herself that that
was what she wanted when she entered the den the
next morning, dragging the heavy duffel bag behind
her. Shane had already arrived. He was standing facing Marty, smiling slightly. Marty, Robyn noted, wore
a defiant, minatory frown.

Abandoning the bag in the doorway, Robyn walked
into the room, saying immediately, "Marty, take that
frown off your face. What have you been saying to
Shane?"

Before Marty could answer, Shane turned to face
Robyn, his warm green eyes sweeping her faded jeans
and full-sleeved pirate blouse. "She was warning me
to take good care of you," he replied. "I told her that
the warning was completely unnecessary." The look
in those emerald eyes brought a flush to Robyn's face.

Trying to ignore her response to that slumbering
green passion, Robyn glanced at Marty. "There was

no need for that," she said uncomfortably. "He isn't kidnapping me, Marty, and I'm not a child!"

"She was worried about you." Shane strode across the room to her side, casually catching her hand in his. "And I don't blame her. You and I haven't known each other very long, after all."

Robyn sneaked a glance at his face but said nothing more as he led her to the door, pausing only long enough to pick up her duffel bag. Marty spoke to Robyn at last, and her voice was perfectly calm. "You two have fun."

Shane smiled winningly at her. "We'll let you know if something delays us. Otherwise, expect Robyn home by Monday."

Robyn barely had time to wave before Shane was tucking her into the black Porsche and stowing her bag in the trunk. Silently, she watched him handle the powerful car for a few moments, then she spoke wryly. "Why do I get the feeling that you tried to charm Marty?"

He grinned unrepentantly, confessing with a theatrical sigh, "It didn't work. She doesn't trust me."

Smiling in spite of herself, Robyn murmured, "I wonder why?"

Wounded, Shane protested, "I'm a prince among men!"

"Put not your trust in princes," she intoned meaningfully.

Shane started laughing, and Robyn reflected briefly that it was good to laugh with someone, good to share a joke or an understanding remark. She felt close to Shane in that moment, and she had to squash her instinctive alarm and remind herself that she was going to have this chance.

Even if it scared her half to death.

When they reached the marina, Shane helped her

from the car, cheerfully reporting that the galley was stocked and everything ready for them. He retrieved her bag from the trunk and carried it for her as they threaded their way through the bewildering maze of boats of every size and description. He finally stopped beside a boat that looked, to Robyn's inexperienced eye, like a battleship. The thing was huge.

Perhaps reading the anxiety in her gaze, Shane assured her, "Don't worry—two can handle it."

"But I don't know anything about sailing," she protested hesitantly, watching him toss her bag aboard and then step neatly onto the deck.

"I'll teach you." Shane appeared unconcerned.

She stared at the hand he held out to her, then mentally burned her bridges. Taking the hand, she made use of the one bit of nautical protocol she'd culled from movies and television. "Permission to come aboard?"

"Granted." He grinned at her, his emerald eyes incredibly bright in the early morning sunlight. He helped her over the side, steadying her as the boat shifted slightly. Robyn suddenly had a horrid thought.

"Oh, no! What if I get seasick?"

He chuckled softly. "I thought of that. There're some pills for motion sickness in the galley. You can take one now, if you like. They really do the trick."

"I think I will," she murmured, releasing her death grip on his hand and bending carefully to pick up her bag. The thought of getting sick drove other thoughts from her mind. She looked toward a doorway and then lifted a quizzical brow at Shane. "Down there?"

"Down there," he confirmed, seemingly amused by her uncertainty. "The galley's to the left when you reach the bottom of the steps. Your cabin's to the right. The galley, by the way, is the kitchen."

Robyn swung the duffel bag over her shoulder and

staggered under the weight of it. Glaring up into his amused eyes, she stated with offended dignity, "I'm not that dumb. I *know* the galley's the kitchen."

She got a firmer grip on her bag and stalked— carefully—toward the doorway. "Are we going to float here all day like a lily pad, or are we going somewhere?" she questioned huffily over her unbur- dened shoulder.

"We're going somewhere," he assured her, laugh- ing. "You put your stuff away and take a pill, then come back up here and give me a hand and we'll get underway."

Robyn went down the steps carefully, leaving her bag in the cubbyhole of a hallway while she explored the galley. The cramped room hardly seemed large enough to store anything in, but she soon discovered that quite a large amount of supplies and foodstuffs had been neatly placed in the cabinets and drawers. She puzzled for a moment over the somewhat elab- orate latches that secured doors and drawers, then realized that such precautions would be necessary in rough seas.

Her already nervous stomach tightened at the re- minder, and she hastily began looking for the motion- sickness pills. She located them in a cabinet over the postage-stamp sized sink. Moments later she had washed down the required number of pills with some orange juice she found in the small refrigerator.

Making sure that everything was again fastened securely, she left the galley. She looked in briefly at the tiny bathroom complete with a narrow shower stall, then opened the remaining door in the hall.

The tiny cubicle, which bore the glorified name of "cabin," was only slightly larger than her closet at home. Two bunk beds took up most of the available room. The remaining space was merely a narrow walkway, lined by the beds on one side and two small chests on the other. Above the chests was a small mirror carefully secured to the wall. Directly opposite the door was a large porthole.

Electing to put her things away later, Robyn lifted her bag to the bottom bunk and then went back out into the hall, shutting the cabin door behind her. She stood there for a moment, knowing there was something bothering her but unable to figure out just what it was. And then she had it.

Separate cabins. He'd said that they would have separate cabins on the trip.

She stared carefully at the three doorways, looked in each room a second time, and then stood in the hall frowning at the steps. Granted, the cabin had two beds. But two beds did not separate cabins make. And Robyn had a feeling that Shane had known exactly how many cabins the boat had before he'd invited her.

Oddly enough, she was more curious to hear his explanation than angry. Climbing to the deck, she blinked in the bright sunlight and briefly took note of the activity going on around them in the marina. Shading her eyes with one hand, she finally located Shane near the front—was that port or starboard, or bow or stern?—of the boat. He'd shed his slacks and stood clothed in a pair of white swim trunks. He was busily engaged in untangling a pile of ropes.

Robyn picked her way carefully along the deck toward him, avoiding more tangles of rope. Reaching his side, she inquired with deliberately deceptive calm, "Weren't we going to try to be friends?"

"Sure." He cast a sidelong look at her, and Robyn had no trouble reading the mischief in his eyes.

"Then tell me something—friend. Why did you lie about there being two cabins on this boat?"

"I didn't exactly lie." He threw her another glance,

then bent his attention back to the rope in his hands. "I said we'd have separate cabins. My cabin's out here; I'll sleep on deck."

"On deck?" she exclaimed as though he'd just proposed sleeping in the ocean. "You can't do that!"

"Why not? The weather's supposed to be fine, and I've certainly slept in worse places."

"But—"

"As a matter of fact, I'll probably be more comfortable than you. The cabin tends to get stuffy at night."

"But—"

Cutting her off smoothly, he murmured, "And you wouldn't want to share the cabin, now, would you?"

Robyn opened her mouth to suggest just that, and then suddenly acquired the suspicion that she was being neatly maneuvered. Beginning to be able to read his expression and subtle body-language, she studied his faint smile and the almost imperceptible tension in his lean body. So he was plotting, was he?

Smiling sweetly, she folded her arms, careful to keep her feet solidly apart on the shifting deck. "I wouldn't think of it," she returned politely. "Why would I deprive you of the pleasure of sleeping out under the stars?"

He turned to look at her, and she nearly giggled at the look of almost comic dismay on his face. "You're not going to let me get away with much, are you?" he murmured wryly.

"Not if I can help it. But don't worry—when this trip's over, you'll be stronger in character." She reached up to give his cheek a friendly pat, and she nearly gasped at the almost electrifying sensation of flesh on flesh. Hurriedly drawing back her hand, she feigned interest in what he was doing with the ropes. "Can I help?" she asked brightly.

He stared at her for a moment, the green eyes strangely dark, then flexed his shoulders abruptly as if throwing off an unwelcome hand...or thought. "No," he muttered, clearing his throat. "No, not right now. We won't be able to raise the sails until we clear the marina. Have a seat in the stern until we're ready to cast off."

Since the only seat she could see—an L-shaped bench—was in the back of the boat, Robyn assumed that that was the stern. Her nerves jumping after the unexpectedly stimulating sensation of touching him, she wasn't about to protest his order. A little shakily, she made her way to the stern and sank down onto the padded bench.

Good Lord, what was wrong with her? She was about to spend several days alone on a boat with a man, and she couldn't even touch him casually without experiencing a heart-stopping shock! She had a funny feeling that their undemanding "friendship" wasn't going to last very long. Her only hope was to keep things light and humorous—and to avoid touching him as much as possible.

Shane had been right—in her case, anyway. Her instincts were in turmoil. After a year of terror for her husband and a year of grief after his death, she had come alive again—extremely so. And she was all too aware of Shane's magnetic, sensual appeal.

Wide-eyed, she watched him moving about the boat, taking note of his catlike grace and sure motions. She remembered his lion's growl, shivering as her nerve endings responded even to the memory, and directed her gaze out over the water.

"Robyn?"

She blinked and jumped in surprise to find Shane standing directly in front of her. "I'm ready," she muttered with clenched-teeth determination, feeling as cheerful as if he'd just announced that the dentist would see her now.

Shane laughed, but his eyes were intent on her face. "Regretting the trip so soon?" he asked softly.

Robyn stood up slowly, all at once aware of the heat of the morning sun, the salty sea breeze, and the curiously vivid green of his eyes. And she wondered why she was wasting time with stupid, useless fears. "No," she responded just as softly. "Not regretting."

A muscle leaped in his lean jaw, and one hand jerked up as though pulled by strings. His fingers hesitated just before touching her cheek, then the hand fell heavily to his side. "Don't look at me like that," he warned roughly. "It plays havoc with all my good intentions!"

"Good intentions?" A smile hovered around the corners of her mouth. "I'll bet this is the first time you've ever denied yourself something you wanted."

He gave her a lopsided grin. "Don't rub it in. And stop smiling at me, you little witch! You have no idea what it does to my blood pressure."

Robyn experienced a sense of wonder at the desire he made no effort to hide, realizing that she'd never in her life met a man who spoke so openly about how he felt.

He reached up to rub his knuckles down her cheek with gentle roughness, then turned her around briskly and gave her a firm swat on the bottom. "Grab that line and cast off when I tell you to!"

Rubbing the abused portion of her anatomy, Robyn threw a half-laughing glare at him over her shoulder and stalked away to take the line he'd indicated. "Aye, aye," she said resentfully. "But please don't ask me to do anything desperately important, skipper, or we'll both end up in the drink!"

Within half an hour, they had left the marina behind. Shane had used the small engine to propel the boat until they were well out, and then cut its power and commanded Robyn to take the wheel while he showed her how to raise the sails.

A bit gingerly, she stood behind the big brass wheel and held it firmly, resisting her desire to watch the colorful sails of other boats heading out to sea. Dutifully, she watched Shane at work, trying to make sense of his movements and not having very much success. She nearly lost him once, swinging the wheel instinctively when a large motorized boat came a bit too close for her peace of mind.

Having regained his balance swiftly, Shane gave her a short lecture on maritime law, which inexplicably proclaimed that the smaller boat had the right of way. Robyn listened meekly.

She felt like a fool until he winked solemnly at her, and she realized that he wasn't at all dismayed by her ignorance. After that, it was easier to absorb his instructions.

"Swing it a bit to port," he called back to her, busily tying off one of the innumerable ropes.

Barely able to hear him over the snapping and cracking of the wind-filled sails, she responded hastily, "You're talking to a landlubber, remember! Is port left or right?"

He laughed. "Sorry! Port's left."

Wary after her near-catastrophe earlier, Robyn carefully turned the wheel to the left and felt rewarded when Shane gave her a thumbs-up signal. She swung her head to throw the single heavy braid back over her shoulder, and reflected that it was a good thing she'd decided on that style this morning. Her fine hair tangled easily, and, without the braid, she would have looked like a wild woman by now.

Apparently satisfied with the sails, Shane made his

way back to her side. He moved deftly and easily about the heaving deck, and Robyn envied him his steady sea legs. She didn't feel sick—yet—but only her death grip on the brass wheel steadied her balance.

She watched him lean against the side of the boat, his arms folded casually across his chest, and she asked uneasily, "Aren't you going to take over now?"

"Why? You're doing fine." Before she could protest, he went on briskly, "We're going to drill a little nautical terminology into your head so you won't panic."

"I never panic," she informed him indignantly.

"Uh huh. Port's left."

Sighing, Robyn realized he wasn't going to let her get out of learning how to sail. Aware that they were far out to sea, and interested in spite of herself, she resolved to learn. "Port's left," she parroted faithfully.

"Starboard's right."

"Starboard's right."

"The front of the boat is the bow, and the rear is the stern. Or you can call it fore and aft—"

"Let's stick with bow and stern," she interrupted quickly. "There's no need to thoroughly confuse me our first day out."

Solemnly, he said, "You have to learn, Robyn. In case something happens to me."

"In case something—" The boat made a decidedly ungentle lurch as her hands jerked on the wheel. "Shane! I can't sail this thing by myself! If you fall out, I'll never forgive you!"

"Overboard," he corrected, his lips twitching.

"What?"

"If I fall overboard. Not out."

She glared at him. "Now, look—"

"Starboard?"

"Right," she supplied irritably. "Shane—"

"Port?"

"Left. Will you—"

"Bow?"

"Front."

"Stern?"

"*Rear*." Her voice held more than a suspicion of gritted teeth.

"Very good," he commended cheerfully. "Think you can remember that much?"

Robyn stared at him for a long moment, then spoke carefully. "Did I ever tell you that I know karate?"

"Nope." His lips twitched again.

"Well, I do. I'm probably a little rusty, but I'm sure I could manage a few lethal moves."

"Should I bear that in mind?"

"I would."

Shane grinned and then sobered abruptly. "I'm not trying to scare you, Robyn. I certainly don't expect any problems between now and Monday. But it's best that you be prepared for anything. You can never take the sea, or the weather, for granted. When we get a little farther out, I'll show you exactly how to raise and lower the sails and the anchor, how to read the compass and handle the radio, and what to do in an emergency." He hesitated and reached out to touch her cheek lightly. "Okay?"

Reassured more by the tingling touch than anything else, she nodded and smiled. "Okay. But don't go too fast!"

"Right." He laughed. "Port?"

"Right. I mean left! Dammit."

"Starboard? . . ."

Two hours later, Robyn had raised and lowered the sails twice by herself, had mastered the peculiar art of hoisting an anchor, was reasonably certain that she could handle the radio, and could make a stab at reading the compass.

She was also hot, tired, aching in more muscles than she'd known she had, and teetering on the brink of telling Shane to forget the whole damn thing.

She collapsed at last onto the cushions of the stern seat, glared at the rope burns on her hands and then at Shane, who was standing comfortably near the big wheel. In the tone of a litany, she recited, "The sails are down, the anchor's in place, we're heading south-by-southwest, and I'm catching the first shore-bound sea gull."

He was laughing at her, dammit!

Trying to infuse her voice with hearty good cheer and succeeding only in sounding weary, she asked, "Anything else, skipper?"

"I think you've done enough, sailor. How about a break?"

Robyn peered at him uncertainly, then sighed with relief when she realized he was being serious. "Oh, thank you," she breathed. "I think I'm dead and you haven't bothered to tell me."

Shane grinned at her. "Don't be ridiculous. Think your stomach could stand some lunch?"

Surprised, Robyn realized that she had been too busy to worry about the possible revolt of her stomach. The gentle rocking motion of the boat wasn't bothering her in the least. "Was that the method to your madness?" she asked suspiciously.

Shane didn't misunderstand. "Partly," he confessed with a grin. "It's a question of mind over matter; if your mind's occupied, the matter generally remains stable. Lunch?"

"Lunch," she agreed. "But only if you fix it."

"That's mutiny!"

"Call it anything you like," she said with a sweet smile.

He sighed dramatically and headed below deck. "It's a good thing I'm a nice guy," he threw over his shoulder at her.

"Attila the Hun probably said the same thing!" she yelled with a final burst of energy. She smiled as she heard Shane's laugh. Glancing around, Robyn was surprised to find that there was no land in sight and the nearest of the colorful sails that had left the marina with them looked miles away. She sincerely hoped that Shane's navigational skills were in order. Her newly acquired compass-reading abilities notwithstanding, she had only the vaguest idea of how to get the boat back to dry land.

The subject of her thoughts came back on deck at that moment, carrying a blanket under one arm and a wicker basket in his free hand. He tossed the blanket at Robyn. "Spread this out on deck while I rig the sun shade. Your nose is getting pink."

"It is not," she automatically countered, spreading the blanket and watching while he stretched an awning over their heads. "I never burn."

"No?" He glanced back at her as he snapped the canvas into place, his green eyes glinting in a smile. "Wrinkle your nose."

She did as he ordered and nearly winced at the tight, prickly feeling of slightly scorched skin. "Well, not much," she amended.

He joined her on the blanket, bringing the hamper with him. "Don't worry, I have some first-aid cream that'll take care of it—and your hands as well. I have a feeling you have some rope burns."

Robyn flexed her hands slightly and smiled at him. "They're a little sore," she admitted, "but not bad."

Shane opened the hamper and began pulling forth goodies from within, a self-satisfied expression on his face that made Robyn instantly suspicious. "Wine, ham and cheese sandwiches, cheese and crackers, assorted fruit, potato salad," he enumerated solemnly.

"You didn't fix this stuff!" she exclaimed. "Where did it come from?"

He grinned at her. "Didn't you see it in the galley? I had the hotel fix it up this morning, and I stored it in the second refrigerator in the galley—where Eric normally keeps his beer."

"Oh." She stared at him, then began dividing the food onto two paper plates while he coped with a stubborn cork. By the time he had opened the wine and poured some of the ruby liquid into two plastic goblets, everything was ready.

Handing her a glass, he lifted his own in a toast. "To friendship," he murmured, a smile playing around the corners of his mouth.

She lifted her glass, softly echoing his words, then sipped carefully, grateful for the drink after her work. She watched him from beneath lowered lashes as they began to eat, wondering at his apparent ability to put the past behind him. Granted, it had been nearly two days since her confession, but he still seemed to have gotten over it awfully quickly. She again inwardly remarked on how little anger he had actually shown.

The only real experience Robyn had had with masculine anger had been with Brian. Her father had been a loving, even-tempered man, and she hadn't been close to any other man except Brian. Brian's reckless temper had been of the long-lasting variety—a deep-freeze of rage that lasted days after the initial explosion.

"You're thinking about him, aren't you?"

She quickly looked down at her wine glass, suddenly afraid that her wayward thoughts had spoiled their trip already. She didn't want Shane to be angry, and she was unable to explain that only the growing and striking contrast between Brian and him had brought her husband to mind.

"Can't you forget about him for a few lousy days?"

There was an odd note in Shane's voice that immediately brought her eyes back to his face. Not anger, but weariness and something that might have been pain quivered in his low tone. And his lean face was so somber that it gave her the courage to speak.

"Shane, the more I get to know you, the more I can't help . . . comparing you to Brian."

He stared down at his half-finished meal, his lips twisted. "Unfavorably?"

"No. Favorably." She smiled a little painfully as his gaze swiftly lifted to hers. "Shane, there were . . . problems in my marriage. Problems that ultimately would have torn it apart, I think. I'll never know for sure. But Brian's gone. He's not a part of my life anymore. Please believe that."

Green eyes now glowing, he stared into her eyes for a long moment, then reached out to clasp her free hand. "Just don't think about him too much, honey," he said softly. "It hurts."

Moved almost beyond bearing by the vulnerability he wasn't afraid to show her, Robyn felt the sting of tears in her eyes. He seemed to care so much, yet they had met less than a week ago.

What did he want from her, this green-eyed man of so many moods? What did he see in her that he was so determined to know her and to have her know him?

He lifted her hand suddenly, rubbing her fingers lightly against his cheek. "Tears?" he queried softly.

"For me?" He shook his head slowly. "Don't cry for me. Not unless I don't get what I want, what I need. In that case, I may join you." Before she could respond, he quickly added, "I'll go get that cream for your burns."

He left her staring after him in wonder.

CHAPTER
Five

ROBYN SLOWLY PUT the lunch things away, knowing that neither of them would finish the meal. She left out only the wine, sipping hers as she tried to understand what had just taken place between her and Shane.

She wasn't quite sure, but she felt that a turning point had somehow been reached and successfully weathered. She didn't think that Shane would be upset again over Brian or her thoughts of him. But Shane, she knew, still had questions about her marriage. And she wasn't certain how to answer the questions when the time came.

She had been honest with Shane—and with herself for the first time. Her marriage to Brian would have been torn apart, either by his eventual infidelity or by her terror of his racing. That didn't mean that she had stopped loving her husband. He would always hold a special place in her heart. He'd been her first love, her first lover; nothing would ever change that. But that was then.

Now she was facing a relationship that could possibly be shadowed—just as her marriage had been—by racing. If she and Shane discovered that they had something special, something to build a future on, then she would have to either conquer her fears or allow them to ruin her life. She would never ask Shane to give up something he loved for her. No matter how dangerous that "something" was.

She would not try to change him.

That resolve had just filtered somewhat painfully into her mind when she heard Shane return and looked up to find him kneeling on the blanket in front of her. He was unscrewing the top of a small tube in his hand and looking at her with smiling eyes.

"The nose first, I think," he said judiciously, and he promptly began smearing some of the white cream across her nose.

Robyn giggled at the cool sensation, but her laughter died when the now-familiar shock tingled over her nerve endings. She stared up at him gravely.

Shane's fingers seemed to quiver slightly as he met her look, and his own emerald gaze became fathoms deep. Somewhat hastily, he finished with her nose and picked up one of her hands, using both of his to work the soothing cream into her reddened palm. He lowered his eyes to the task, and she could have sworn that he caught his breath.

The movements of his fingers over first one palm and then the other were strangely erotic, causing a trembling to start deep inside her, spreading outward until her fingers shook within his. She could feel her heart thudding against her rib cage and wondered dimly if he was aware of the pulse pounding in her wrist.

The cream disappeared into her skin, and still his fingers continued their gentle stroking, caressing. Without looking up at her, he said very quietly, "I had to touch you. You realize that, don't you?"

The soft statement made her thudding heart skip a beat. She tried to swallow the lump in her throat, her eyes searching his face as though it held the secrets of the universe. Still he refused to look at her. When he went on, his voice had deepened, hoarsened.

"I've tried to keep my hands off you all morning and haven't succeeded worth a damn. I *have* to touch you, Robyn. The same way I have to breathe. Don't hate me for that."

"I don't hate you, Shane."

He looked up at last as she whispered the denial, and his hands closed convulsively around hers with a gentle, savage strength. His eyes were nearly black. "Don't look at me like that, dammit," he swore softly. "Even when you don't mean to, you look at me with bedroom eyes!"

"Who says I don't mean to?" she managed shakily.

His eyes flared with emerald fire, and he released her hands to cradle her face with his large palms. "Honey, you don't know what you're saying. We're supposed to be getting to know each other as friends."

"I know." She reached up to grasp his wrists, suddenly understanding his statement about needing to touch her. She needed to touch him, desperately, almost painfully. It was like a hunger eating away at her soul. Bewildered by the strength of that need, the throbbing emptiness inside her, she pleaded huskily, "Please don't think I'm a tramp, Shane! I—I need you to touch me, I want you to! I can't help it..."

He abruptly rose on his knees, releasing her face to pull her up against his body, wrapping his arms around her firmly. "Of course I don't think you're a tramp!" he scolded unevenly. "You're confused, honey; everything's happened too fast. I just want you to be very, very sure of what you feel."

She intuitively sensed he was holding something back. What were the words he didn't speak, she wondered dimly, slipping her arms around his lean waist with a need beyond reason. Was he afraid that she still saw him as a replacement for Brian? Was he still thinking of another man's ghost?

Shane drew back far enough to gaze down at her face, his own very serious. "I want nothing less than a commitment from you, Robyn, and I don't think you're ready for that yet."

Unbidden, she thought of his racing, and a stab of fear shot through her. The fear must have been reflected in her eyes, and Shane obviously misinterpreted what he saw there.

He drew away suddenly, getting to his feet. "You see?" He smiled reassuringly, softening the blow of his taut voice. "You're scared to death of committing yourself to me, honey. You aren't ready for that yet."

Robyn wanted to voice another denial, but she couldn't work up the courage. Then the moment had passed, and it was too late.

"Give me a hand, and we'll get underway," he was saying lightly. "I'd like to reach Key Largo this afternoon."

Clamping a lid over the turmoil of her emotions, Robyn silently set about helping him to get the boat underway. Once they were skimming over the blue-green sea again, she left Shane at the wheel, gathered up the remains of their lunch, and went below.

She put everything in its place and then went into her cabin, emptied her duffel bag on the bottom bunk, and began putting her things away in one of the chests. The other chest, she noted, held Shane's clothing.

She resisted an impulse to run her fingers through his things, telling herself firmly not to be an idiot.

And then, unable to delay the moment any longer, she changed into a pair of cut-off jeans and a very brief halter top and went back up on deck—to the man who would or would not become her future.

Shane was standing behind the wheel. He watched her until she sat down on the padded bench, a lambent flame flickering for a moment in the depths of his eyes. Then he was paying attention to their course again.

"Have you ever seen the living coral reef off Key Largo?" he asked casually.

Robyn drew one foot up on the bench and hugged her knee, watching him. "No. Will we see it?"

"If we get there in time today, we can tie up nearby and take a ride in a glass-bottomed boat. How does that sound?"

"Great." She frowned slightly. "Tie up? Won't we just drop the anchor?"

"We'll tie up in the marina tonight, since we'll be leaving the boat. And once we reach Key West, too. In between, we'll just drop anchor in some little cove."

"Swim and fish?" A smile played over her lips.

He sent her a quick, answering smile. "Sure. I wouldn't advise swimming out here in the open sea, but the coves should be safe enough. Have you ever fished?"

"Years ago, but never in the ocean. I'll just watch you."

"That won't be any fun."

Silently, she thought: That's what you think! Aloud, she murmured, "How long does it take to get to Key Largo?"

"A couple of hours, if the wind holds."

A companionable silence fell between them. She

joined him in staring out to sea, wondering what he was thinking and trying to make sense of her own thoughts. When he finally spoke, she almost wished he hadn't.

"Do I really look so much like him?"

Robyn felt her fingernails biting into her arms and had to make a conscious effort to relax. "Not really. He was dark but blue-eyed. And you're taller." When Shane turned his head to meet her steady gaze, she repeated, "Not really."

"Tell me about him. How you met."

She hesitated, staring at him. "Shane—"

"I have to know, Robyn."

Robyn stared down at her knee for a moment, then told him what she could. "We met at a party..." She looked up quickly, wishing she could recall the words, but Shane showed no reaction other than a slight frown. Hastily, she went on.

"My father had died recently, and I wasn't really used to going out much. But I was attracted to Brian. He always seemed to be smiling. We dated for a few months. He traveled quite a bit in his...work." She took a breath and finished calmly, "He asked me to marry him and—and I accepted."

"You don't like talking to me about your husband, do you?" he asked quietly.

"No," she replied honestly.

"Why not?"

"Because I'm afraid." The stark words were out before she could halt them, and they had to be explained. "I'm afraid you believe that I'm seeing Brian whenever I look at you, and that's not true. And I don't want you to see Brian's ghost every time you look at me."

Staring straight ahead, Shane told her huskily, "When I look at you, honey, I see *you*. I see a beautiful woman whose life I very badly want to be a part of. If there were ten men in your past, a dozen ghosts at your side, it wouldn't matter."

Robyn took a deep, shaky breath. "Then can we put the subject behind us? At least during the trip?"

He nodded, automatically glancing down to check their direction by the compass and then swinging the brass wheel slightly to starboard. "We'll put it behind us," he agreed.

This time, the companionable silence stretched for nearly an hour, broken only by an occasional comment. Robyn was enjoying the sound of the wind snapping the sails, the steady slapping of water against the hull, and the feel of the salt spray in her face.

A pair of dolphins joined them as Key Largo came into sight, and Robyn was completely entranced by their antics. The beautiful mammals leaped in and out of the blue-green sea, bright black eyes seeming to invite the watching humans to join their game. Robyn laughed in delight as their friendly escorts stood up on their tails and chattered gaily, clearly wishing their observers a fond good-bye before heading rapidly back out to sea.

She stared after them, unaccountably wistful. "Oh, Shane, aren't they beautiful?" she marveled.

"Beautiful," he confirmed softly.

But she saw he wasn't looking at the dolphins.

They spent the remainder of the afternoon exploring, leaving the boat tied up in the marina. They put the past behind them and threw off the trappings of dignity and caution. Cheerfully, they became more and more childlike as the day wore on, each trying to top the other and stretching toward the heights of absurdity.

Shane solemnly told the other tourists on the glass-bottomed boat that his companion was his niece, home from school for the holidays, and he earned dubious looks from his listeners as they took in Robyn's somewhat revealing halter top and shorts. Robyn stared back at them, wide-eyed, and slowly blew a bubble with the gum Shane had bought her only moments before.

She got even with him sometime later, telling the owner of a small tourist shop they wandered into that she was being kidnapped and would shortly be sold into white slavery. The ploy wasn't very effective, however, since Shane was playfully leading her around by her braid.

The shopkeeper, with an expression that clearly said he'd heard it all, watched bemusedly as the "kidnapper" bought his "slave" a stuffed dolphin and a book on sailing. The odd couple was still arguing spiritedly over who needed a book on sailing as they wandered out.

They located a hot dog stand near the marina and elected to stop there for a casual supper after Robyn flatly refused to try cooking on the boat.

"I'm not even sure I can light that stove," she declared.

"We agreed to share the galley duty!"

"Well, you haven't done your share yet. You cheated with lunch."

"I never cheat—"

"So I'll cheat with supper," she interrupted firmly, sniffing at the delicious aroma of bubbling chili. She tucked her blue and white dolphin under one arm and smiled at Shane sunnily.

He gave her much-abused braid a tug. "You should be keelhauled!"

"What's that mean? They're always threatening that in pirate movies."

"It means something terrible. Fatal, in fact."

"Then you can't keelhaul me. I'm your only crew."

Shane gave her a long-suffering look, tucked the small paperback on sailing into the waistband of his slacks, and reached for his wallet. "Uh huh. Tell the man what you want on your hot dog."

"What's he got? Let's see . . ."

Ten minutes later, they were seated on a bench near the hot dog stand finishing their supper. Robyn licked one finger clean and said thoughtfully. "Hot dogs are like pizza and spaghetti—impossible to eat with any dignity."

"To hell with dignity," Shane replied indistinctly, reaching for his soft drink to wash down the last bite.

"Dignity is important," she objected in the tone of one looking forward to a good argument.

"Only when meeting kings and presidents."

"And prospective in-laws." Robyn wished that she could call back the comment, and added hurriedly, "And policemen."

"Doctors, lawyers, Indian chiefs?" he murmured, casting her a sidelong smiling look.

Robyn pretended she hadn't said that about in-laws. She explained apologetically, "It probably comes of being raised by a career-army father. I have a phobia about authority figures."

Shane crumpled up his hot dog wrapper and shot it neatly into a nearby trash can. "Any other phobias I should know about?" he asked politely.

"Well . . . there's my fear of water—"

"*What?*"

"I'm kidding, I'm kidding!" She jumped up hastily, swinging her braid out of his reach. "Oh, no, you don't! If you pull on that braid one more time, I'll be bald!"

"Come here, you little witch!" He got to his feet, advancing toward her purposefully.

Robyn clutched her dolphin in front of her like a shield and cast harried, mock-fearful looks around her. But they were interrupted before Shane could wreak vengeance on her.

"Aren't you Shane Justice?"

Both of them turned instinctively as two teenaged girls approached them, beaming happily at Shane and totally ignoring Robyn. They wore cut-off jeans and T-shirts with NASCAR emblazoned in bold black print across jutting breasts. Robyn wasn't the slightest bit surprised to find racing fans here. She'd seen them in stranger places.

The girls were pelting Shane with questions about his racing, barely letting him get a word in and giving him no opportunity to introduce Robyn. More amused by Shane's embarrassment than irritated by the interruption, Robyn quietly gathered up the remains of their supper and made a short trip to the trash can. She returned to his side just as the girls were happily telling Shane that they were in Florida for the race and were heading toward Daytona the next day. Of course, they'd see him there.

Robyn took another good look at them and admitted to herself that she'd been wrong about their ages. The blonde was quite possibly her own age, and the brunette only slightly younger. And both were looking at Shane with eyes that ate him alive.

"Could we have your autograph?" the brunette asked, producing a felt-tipped pen and turning her back so that Shane could sign her T-shirt. He did so, politely.

The blonde was made of sterner stuff. When Shane turned to her she threw back her long hair and stuck out her chest with what appeared to Robyn to be excessive pride. "Over the 'a'," she murmured seductively, gazing into his startled eyes.

Robyn rested her chin on the nose of her dolphin and bit back a laugh as she watched the red creep up into Shane's cheeks. He obviously tried not to touch the blonde's ample gifts with anything but the pen. At the last possible moment, however, the blonde inhaled, and Shane's signature ended in a rather peculiar scrawl. He hastily returned the pen to the brunette.

The blonde finally looked at Robyn with speculative eyes. "Are you his sister?" she asked sweetly. "Or his maiden aunt?"

Robyn wasn't about to let her get away with that! She quickly grasped Shane's arm and rubbed her cheek against his shoulder adoringly. "Actually, I'm his mistress," she confided gently.

The brunette gasped as though her idol had just developed a bad case of clay feet. The blonde continued to smile, however forced it may have been. "Really?" she asked disbelievingly.

"Oh, yes." Robyn's voice was still soft and gentle, but her cool eyes met the narrowing blue gaze of the other with more than a hint of warning. "I practically never leave his side."

The dueling match of eyes continued for a long moment. Ultimately the blonde turned away, saying meaningfully over her shoulder, "See you in Daytona, Shane!" Her friend hurried after her.

Robyn released Shane's arm, acquiring a firmer grip on her slipping dolphin, and looked up at her silent companion. "Groupies?" she asked innocently.

"Sorry," he murmured, staring down at her with an odd expression. "Racing fans are . . . fans."

"Short for fanatic, I assume." She didn't like that

considering look on his face. "Uh, the sun's going down. Shouldn't we head back toward the boat?"

He didn't move. "You were very convincing with that possessive act, Robyn."

She wasn't about to answer the question he hadn't asked. "Did it bother you?" she asked lightly.

He shook his head slowly. "I'm just wondering why you went to the trouble," he said very softly.

"No trouble at all," she responded flippantly, adding easily, "Isn't the marina this way?" Determinedly, she headed off. Within a few steps, Shane had silently joined her. He remained silent until they had nearly reached the already lighted marina.

Robyn was caught up in her own thoughts, emotions, and sensations. Both her hand and her cheek were still tingling from the brief contact with Shane, and she was belatedly astonished by the surge of possessive rage she had felt when that blonde had looked at Shane with proprietary eyes. She had wanted to do much more than sweetly warn away the other woman. What she had wanted to do was to drop her dolphin, launch herself at the blonde's throat, and engage in a grade-A, number-one catfight.

To a woman who had never lifted her hand against another person in anger, that desire was as shocking as it was totally unfamiliar.

"Penny for your thoughts."

Hastily dragging her mind from its contemplation of the latest in a series of unfamiliar sensations, Robyn responded briefly, "They're not worth that."

"Robyn, if those fans upset you—"

"No, of course not," she interrupted, resisting her impulse to look up at him. She knew that Shane was puzzled by her suddenly guarded mood, but she wasn't about to explain that she was disturbed by primitive emotions she had never experienced before. That confession would ultimately lead to the one she was as yet unprepared to make. She was not ready to tell Shane that she loved him.

He sighed. "You're baffling, do you know that? Every time I think I have you figured out, you change moods on me. Is it a game to you, Robyn?"

She stopped walking suddenly and looked up at him, able to see him clearly in the harsh light from the marina. "No. Shane . . . let's don't spoil the day. Please? With—with soul-searching, or whatever. It's been fun, and I . . . Don't spoil it."

He gazed down at her for a moment, and she saw a muscle tighten in his jaw. Then he was smiling. "Okay, witch," he said lightly. "We won't spoil anything."

Relieved, Robyn started toward the walkway leading down to the boats, but a sudden commotion halted her in her tracks. A royally groomed and beribboned poodle was dashing toward them, barking hysterically. In front of the poodle ran a scrawny black cat with wild yellow eyes and a crooked tail. The dog was gaining.

Robyn thrust the stuffed dolphin at Shane and, as the cat started to run between them, she snatched it up into her arms. The dog, dodging Shane's instinctive swipe with the dolphin, turned tail and ran.

Shane turned immediately to Robyn. "Honey, turn it loose—it looks as mad as a hatter! The dog's gone."

But his obvious fears that the cat would scratch or bite Robyn were completely misplaced. Thin sides heaving and tail twitching erratically, the animal made no move to struggle.

"The poor thing! Look, Shane, its ear's all torn." She gently fingered one tattered ear. "Its coat's all matted, and I can feel every rib—"

"Robyn," Shane broke in patiently, "we can't take a cat with us on the boat. We'll find someone—"

"It's hungry!"

"—to take care of it," he finished firmly.

"It might be sick!"

"All the more reason—"

"Every boat needs a mascot. And it doesn't have a home; I just know it doesn't. It wouldn't take up much room."

"Robyn—"

"I'll take care of it!"

"Robyn, you can't paper-train a cat!"

She looked up at him pleadingly. "We can work something out. Please, Shane?"

"Oh, hell," he muttered. "You're more trouble than you're worth, do you know that?"

"Am I?"

He stared at her, then gruffly answered, "No." He handed her the dolphin, turned her toward the walkway, and gave her a light swat on the bottom. "Go on to the boat. I'll see if I can rustle up a litter box and some cat food."

Robyn smiled at him over her shoulder as he strode off into the darkness, then made her way carefully to the boat. Luckily, the marina was somewhat thin of boats at the moment, so she had very little trouble finding theirs.

On board, she went below and turned on the battery-powered lights in the galley. She rummaged around until she located a can of tuna for her new pet. While the cat—a "he" she had discovered—was eating, she went into her cabin and left the dolphin on the bunk, then found her spare hairbrush, her shampoo, and a towel.

The cat didn't like the small galley sink. Nor did

he enjoy having every inch of his emaciated self ruthlessly washed. He was, however, remarkably docile about the situation. He never once threatened to scratch or bite.

Robyn dried him carefully with the towel, talking to him all the while, and fed him another small meal of condensed milk. When Shane returned nearly an hour later, she was sitting cross-legged on the floor of the galley, gently applying peroxide to one battered ear of a hesitantly purring and much-improved-looking black cat.

"Got it tamed, I see." He set a plastic box and two bags on the tiny table. "It looks like you've made a friend for life."

"He doesn't look so bad now, does he?" Robyn inquired in a rewarded voice, putting the top back on the peroxide bottle. "In a week or so, he'll be a new cat!"

Shane sat down on the narrow bench by the table. "He, huh? Well, what are you going to name him?"

"I don't know. Suggestions?"

"Pyewacket," Shane supplied instantly.

Robyn started laughing. "Why that?"

"Because he's obviously going to be a witch's familiar."

"Funny, funny. Be serious!"

"King George, then."

Robyn cocked her head to one side. "Which King George?" she asked gravely.

"The one they had to lock up."

"George III?"

"If that's the one they had to lock up. He was mad as a hatter, too. Kept screaming 'Off with their heads!'"

Robyn frowned at him. "I think you're a little confused. The Queen of Hearts in *Alice in Wonderland* screamed that. King George III was just a little batty."

Shane's emerald eyes twinkled down at her. "If you say so. Anyway, that's a King George if ever I saw one."

"Have you?"

"Have I what?"

"Ever seen one?"

"Don't be so literal."

Robyn grinned at him, then sobered abruptly. "Thank you for letting me keep him, Shane." She looked down at the sleepy cat in her lap. "I've never been able to have a pet before."

"Why not?"

She waved a hand vaguely, still watching the cat. "Oh, Daddy traveled so much, from base to base. It just wasn't practical. And Brian had an allergy."

"So you compromised."

"I suppose." Robyn was dimly surprised that both she and Shane were beginning to take any mention of her husband so calmly. Shane no longer tensed whenever Brian was mentioned, and Robyn found herself a little less guarded.

"You've always compromised for the men in your life, haven't you, honey?" he suggested quietly.

Robyn looked up, startled. "I don't know what you mean," she said uncertainly.

"I think you do." Shane was watching her very intently. He shifted sideways on the bench, leaning forward and resting his elbows on his knees. "You traveled with your father, even though I'm willing to bet you never enjoyed it. You didn't have a pet because it would have been a problem for him."

"I traveled with Daddy because I wanted to be with him," Robyn insisted quietly. "My mother died when I was three; Daddy was all I had. And he never refused to get me a pet."

"Because you never asked."

More than a little startled by Shane's perception, Robyn could only stare at him mutely. He went on, his voice determined.

"Then there was your husband. I think you compromised a great deal with him. You said that he traveled a lot in his work—and you traveled with him. He had an allergy, so you didn't have a pet. And I'll bet you didn't work because he didn't want you to."

"I didn't have to work."

"But you wanted to. I'm sure you went to college. Business degree?"

She nodded slowly, her gaze dropping to the sleeping cat.

"You wanted to work, maybe start your own business. But your husband didn't want you to. So you didn't."

"Make your point, Shane," she said in a low voice, tacitly admitting that his guesses were on target.

"You're a very…selfless woman, Robyn. You always seem to be molding yourself to someone else's wishes. Even this trip. The thought of getting involved with me threw you into a panic, but you agreed rather than fight me."

"Would you rather I'd said no?" she snapped suddenly, looking up at him with stormy eyes.

"There it is," he said softly, as if to himself. "That spark of temper. How much you must have resented doing what was best for someone else instead of what was best for you."

"You didn't answer my question, Shane," she pointed out tightly.

He smiled slightly, his green eyes still thoughtful. "You know the answer. I'm very glad you said yes. But, Robyn, don't ever hesitate to get mad at me, or tell me what you really think. It's very important for you and me to be honest with each other. Agreed?"

Robyn got to her feet slowly, holding King George in her arms. Shane was so patient, she thought wonderingly, so determined to set their relationship on the right course. "It's been a long day. I think I'll take a shower and turn in. Good night, Shane."

"Agreed, Robyn?" he repeated firmly.

"Agreed," she murmured at last, heading toward her cabin.

She put King George on her bunk and watched the cat curl himself into a contented ball, then she gathered up some things and went into the tiny bathroom. She coped with the narrow shower stall almost automatically, her mind occupied with what Shane had said. Emerging from the bathroom minutes later, she found that he had fixed the litter box for George and left it in the hallway. She was at her cabin door, wearing her terry robe and carrying odds and ends, when Shane stuck his head out of the galley.

"I got my sleeping bag and some other stuff from the cabin, so I won't have to disturb you later. Good night, honey." The emerald eyes flared slightly as they took in the damp robe, but he said nothing more.

Robyn murmured a good night and went into her cabin, shutting the door quietly behind her. She sat on her bunk for a long time, watching George with eyes that never really saw him.

Shane was right: they had to be honest. In theory, that was fine. But in practice...

She could never be truly honest with Shane, she knew, until he was told who and what her husband had been. Until he knew how terrified she was of giving her heart to another reckless man...

CHAPTER
Six

GEORGE CLAIMED HIS new role of ship's cat with great gusto and rapidly learned certain key words of nautical terminology. Phrases such as "You damned cat!" irately bellowed at him by Shane while Robyn laughed obviously meant that sail-climbing wasn't encouraged.

Robyn tried her best to teach the seagoing cat a few manners, but he seemed obstinately determined to get on Shane's nerves. In fact, as Shane pointed out menacingly, he seemed to have a death wish. Robyn spent most of Thursday alternately yelling at the cat and warning Shane not to yell at the cat. She finally pointed out to George that swimming back to land wasn't something to look forward to, but since her pet chose to ignore the lecture in order to attack the end of a line Shane was tying off, she couldn't feel that she had done much good.

"Robyn!"

"I know, I know! George, don't do that! Maybe if I wrap you up in one of these ropes, you'll stop playing with them."

"I'm going to tie him to the anchor and drop him overboard!"

"You wouldn't do that to a defenseless creature—"

"Defenseless? He scratched the hell out of me not an hour ago!"

"You pulled his tail!"

"How else was I supposed to get him down from the sail? Now look at him, dammit! You stupid cat, that's a mast not a tree!"

"Shane, don't—" She listened to words of blue origin for a moment, then murmured, "—pull his tail."

"Robyn, I'm warning you—!"

"All right, all right! I'll get him down."

When she wasn't saving George from the jaws of death or becoming an accomplished sailor, Robyn spent most of her time trying to learn how to work the stove in the galley. Shane had fixed breakfast— and very well, too. Lunch had been sandwiches, but supper had to be cooked. Robyn was elected.

The stove was a gas model, and the pilot kept going out. Being just a bit wary of fires on boats at sea, Robyn kept yelling for Shane to come down and light it for her. After his fifth patient trip below deck, Robyn noticed a somewhat frantic gleam in his eyes, and she decided prudently to handle the stove by herself from then on.

She pulled out all the stops with supper, determined to give Shane the best meal he'd ever had on land *or* sea. The boat was anchored in a small cove near Long Key, and Shane was topside getting everything ready for night, so other than stepping over George every time she turned around, Robyn was able to work undisturbed.

She delved into her memory for Marty's cooking lessons and produced a meal that even that stern critic would have praised. Ruthlessly making use of all the fresh vegetables Shane had stocked, she fixed a savory stew, the heavenly aroma of which made her mouth water. She took advantage of the cook's privilege of "tasting" and managed to stave off starvation while completing the rest of the meal.

The stew was to be accompanied by creamed corn, a crisp green salad, and biscuits made from a special southern recipe. She also found a can of apples and managed to make an apple pie in spite of the oven's recalcitrance.

She was hot, tired, and smudged with flour by the time she yelled for Shane to come and get it. The expression of surprise on his face, however, made up for her weariness. But she became more than a little irritated by his unflattering astonishment when he tasted the first bite.

"My word. She can cook!"

"Well, you don't have to look so surprised."

"How was I to know? You seem to be a lily of the field when it comes to everything else."

Robyn picked up her fork and glared at him. "Can you walk on water?" she asked with deceptive mildness.

"No," he replied, eyeing her warily.

"Then you'd better quit while you've still got a boat underfoot."

"Sorry." Shane bent his attention to the meal and was silent for a few moments. Soon he began murmuring, "This is terrific . . . I haven't eaten a meal this good in years . . . spices and everything . . . Is that an apple pie I smell?"

Robyn finally looked up at him with laughing eyes. "All right, you can stop now! I've been suitably mollified. Besides, I didn't rave like that over your bacon and eggs."

"Those weren't worthy of raving. This is." He grinned at her, then stood to get himself another helping of stew.

After the pie, they shared the cleaning-up chores, which soon became a comical enterprise in the cramped quarters—particularly since George insisted on getting into the act. George retired to the cabin, however, after Shane stepped on his tail for the second time.

By the time the last dish was washed and put away, Robyn was beginning to feel more than a little breathless at Shane's nearness. Aloud, she blamed the stuffiness of the galley and quickly climbed the steps to the deck for some air.

She stared out over the sea, listening to the gentle slapping of water against the hull and the night sounds coming from the tiny island a few yards away. When Shane came up behind her and pulled her back against him in a gentle embrace, she didn't resist.

He rested his chin on the top of her head. "I've enjoyed today," he murmured softly, as though reluctant to disturb the peace all around them.

Robyn smiled into the darkness. "Even George?"

"Even George." He pulled her a bit closer, then added whimsically, "Do you know that you have a smudge of flour on your nose?"

"And you're just now telling me about it?"

"I think it's cute. Adds a certain something."

"I'm sure!" Robyn reached up to wipe the smudge away, but Shane turned her around to face him.

"No, let me."

Robyn looked up at him, able to see him now in the glow from the huge yellow moon rising over the horizon. She felt the tingling shock of his fingers softly brushing over her nose, and she became suddenly, painfully aware of a churning emptiness in the pit of her belly. Without conscious volition, her hand lifted to rest lightly on his chest, feeling the springy softness of curling hair exposed by the opening of his shirt.

Shane's brushing fingers began to caress, tracing the curve of her cheek, the trembling softness of her lips, finally cupping her face warmly. His free hand lifted to her hair, raking through it gently and freeing the heavy mass from the pins she had used to keep it out of her way.

"I want you so much," he breathed huskily.

Robyn was sure the fingers lightly touching her throat could feel her pounding pulse, but she didn't care. "You made up the rules," she whispered. "You have all the good intentions."

"Would you have come with me if I hadn't decided on the rules and the good intentions?" he asked roughly.

"I . . . don't know," Robyn answered honestly. "But I think I would have."

Shane's hand slid down her back abruptly, pulling her lower body against his and making her all too aware of his pulsing desire. "Robyn, you're driving me out of my mind!" he groaned hoarsely. "How can I keep my hands off you when you say things like that?"

Robyn was very tired of conversation. She slipped her arms up around his neck, standing on tiptoe to mold her body against his. "I don't know," she murmured. "Tell me."

"Robyn . . ." His mouth unerringly found hers in a

fierce kiss of driving need. It was like that first night, when nothing seemed to matter but their mutual desire, their need to touch and go on touching because it was something they couldn't fight.

Along with the excitement fluttering through her veins, Robyn felt a sense of triumph and exhilaration. She was tired of playing by Shane's rules, and more than a little dissatisfied with the platonic relationship he had imposed on them. Unwilling to make a commitment, she was still fiercely determined to be in his arms, to feel his touch on her reawakened body. She wanted him.

Her fingers threaded through his hair, her mouth echoing his demand with a heat that matched his own. Shane's hands moved up and down her back unsteadily, shaping her willing flesh and pulling her closer until their hearts seemed to beat with a single pounding rhythm.

Robyn threw her head back, shivering, as his mouth finally left hers to press hot kisses against her throat. Through half-closed eyes, she stared up at the stars, thinking dimly that they had never seemed so close. She could almost reach out and touch them.

"Robyn, you're playing with fire," Shane warned hoarsely, his hands defying the protest with increasingly demanding caresses.

She gasped when one hand closed around a sensitized breast, forgetting the stars for more earthly things. She could feel his thumb probing through the material of her knit top, and she managed to say fiercely, breathlessly, "I hope I get burned!"

Quite suddenly, her upper arms were gripped in steely hands, and she was held nearly a foot away from the body she wanted so badly to touch. Shane was staring down at her, his jaw taut, his eyes a glittering neon green in the moonlight.

"But *I* don't want to be the one to burn you. Don't you understand that?" he asked hoarsely. "I don't want to wake up in the morning and find you gone because you only needed one night. I need *more* than one night, dammit! And until I'm sure—"

Robyn broke the grip of his hands and took a careful step backward. For the first time, she was furious with him. Utterly and completely furious. He was trying to back her into a corner, and she didn't like it one damn bit!

She was only dimly aware that there was a curious role reversal in the situation. She was taking the "traditional" male attitude, insisting on no strings and no complications. She wouldn't make a commitment while the threat of his hobby haunted her. But Shane wanted more.

Robyn didn't say a word as she turned and made her way to the top of the steps. There she spun about abruptly to face him. "Tell me something," she requested, her voice amazingly mild under the circumstances. "How many times do I have to throw myself at you before you catch me?"

With his back to the rising moon, she could make out nothing of his expression. But his silhouette was stiff with tension, and she could see that his hands were clenched into fists at his sides. When he answered her question, his voice was a hoarse rasp in the darkness.

"As many times as it takes. Until you get it right."

Robyn's smile showed most of her teeth but was not meant to be taken as amusement. "I'll keep that in mind."

She turned back to the steps, making her way down them to the hall. Going into her cabin, she flipped on the light, shut the door with unnatural care, and then looked around for something to throw across the tiny room. The only thing she found was her pillow, and that made a disappointingly quiet thump against the wall.

She ducked under the top bunk to sit on the lower one, leaning against the wall and staring with brooding eyes at the small chests containing her and Shane's clothing.

How, she wondered vaguely, did one go about seducing a man?

Oddly enough, she had never had the opportunity to employ such tactics, and she hadn't the faintest idea how to go about the thing. And there was no one to ask advice of. She couldn't very well radio the Coast Guard and ask them to find someone to give her a verbal crash course in the art of seduction.

She should have asked that blonde...

The thoughts and speculation that sailed lazily through Robyn's mind during the next hour surprised her. She was tired of playing Shane's games, but her determination to play a game of her own struck her as being not only odd but also potentially dangerous. It would be much simpler to just go up to Shane, announce that she was ready to make a commitment, and then attack him.

Robyn chuckled as that scene played out in her mind's eye, then she sobered. She couldn't do that. Maybe because she wanted to put off facing what had to be faced—his damned racing.

In the meantime, however, her nerve endings were shrieking at her, and she had a feeling she wouldn't sleep tonight. Her body cried out for Shane. Slightly less than a week before, he had shown her delights she didn't want to have to do without.

Yet for some reason, she was determined to have

what she wanted without having to commit herself. Perhaps it had something to do with Shane's calling her "selfless."

For once in her life, she was going to be selfish. So all right. She chewed on a knuckle thoughtfully. Intuition told her that if she wandered up on deck stark naked and started talking casually about the weather, she would probably accomplish what she wanted.

That, however, would hardly be subtle. In fact, it would be downright blatant. Even if she could find the nerve for it.

She slid from the bunk and stepped over to her chest, opening drawers and taking out an item now and then. Funny . . . she might almost have had seduction in mind when she'd packed for this nice platonic trip. And even if Shane suspected what she was up to, there wasn't very much he could do about it. So she had until Sunday night to accomplish her "task." By Monday afternoon, they'd be back in Miami, and Shane would be on his way to Daytona.

Three days . . .

When Robyn entered the galley on Friday morning, Shane was busily making pancakes and George was sitting beneath the tiny table with an aggrieved expression on his furry face.

"You've been stepping on George's tail again, haven't you?" Robyn demanded in lieu of a more traditional good morning.

"He got in my way." Shane cast an irritated glance at their feline mascot. "That's probably how his tail got to be crooked in the first place." He half turned to look at Robyn, and his eyes widened almost comically as they swept her petite figure, which was clad only—apparently—in a dark green button-up shirt that belonged to him.

"I borrowed a shirt of yours," she said casually. "Hope you don't mind." She could see his eyes speculating on whether or not she wore anything beneath the flimsy cotton.

"Not at all," he muttered, turning back to the stove.

Robyn smiled slightly as she gazed at his broad back. The smile was new to her, something that had surprised her only moments before while she'd looked into the mirror and brushed her hair. Her smile, she had realized, was feline in the extreme. The way she imagined women down through the ages must have smiled while busily plotting the downfall of a man . . .

"Can I help?" she asked brightly.

"Feed your cat," he grunted.

Robyn crossed to his side to open a cabinet door. "My, but we're surly this morning," she observed, getting out the cat food. "Didn't we sleep well?"

Shane neatly flipped a pancake out of the pan and onto a plate. "Since neither one of us is royalty," he said tersely, "you can dispense with the 'we.' *I* slept fine."

Since Robyn had heard him pacing the deck above her head long after she'd turned out her light, she knew that to be a barefaced lie. But she hid another smile and silently fed her cat.

She was encouraged rather than upset by his irritation. It showed her clearly that his good intentions were beginning to get a bit threadbare. And that was just fine with her.

They ate breakfast in something of a strained silence, then Shane went up on deck to get them underway while Robyn cleaned up the galley. By the time she mounted the steps, he was ready to raise the sails.

Robyn took the wheel, watching him and humming to herself. Her hair, not braided or pinned up today, fanned out behind her in the breeze as the boat began moving in the brisk wind.

It was oppressively hot even with the wind, and the sky looked a bit hazy. Robyn saw Shane cast several thoughtful glances up while he worked, but he said nothing.

Shane shed his shirt and tossed it back to land at Robyn's feet, leaving him only in shorts and sneakers. She inhaled deeply at the magnificent spectacle. She saw him glance back at her more than once, but what was on his mind she couldn't tell. He came to take the wheel once they were well underway, and she stepped back with a smile.

He returned the smile—half forced and half wary, Robyn thought—but the expression died an almost ludicrous death when she calmly started unbuttoning her shirt.

"Robyn—"

"I think I'll get some sun," she said casually. "Is it too hazy, do you think?" She tossed the shirt onto the padded bench.

Shane's eyes swept her body, taking in the bathing suit that would have turned heads on the Riviera, and then skittered away hastily. "No," he rasped, and then cleared his throat. "No, I don't think it's too hazy. Watch out that you don't burn, though."

"I'll be careful," she promised, leaning against the side of the boat and reaching back to brace herself on the low chrome railing. The suit, she thought cheerfully, certainly had the effect the saleslady had promised.

It was black, one-pieced, and far from demure. Tying at the neck, two narrow strips came down to just barely cover the tips of her small full breasts before joining below her navel, becoming one strip that continued between her thighs and back up over the gentle swell of her bottom. Two skimpy strings anchored the bottom part of the suit by tying around her waist.

The strings were tied in a bow.

Robyn had bought the suit on a whim—mainly because Kris had been teasing her—and had never gotten up the nerve to wear it. Until now.

She was feeling reckless, and the feeling was wonderful. She felt marvelously free for the first time in literally years, pleasing herself by deciding to tempt the fates and do something out of character. If she had been playing with fire the night before, she was playing with dynamite now, and there was something wild and exhilarating about it.

In that moment, Robyn came closer than she ever had to understanding why men like Shane and Brian shared a love of danger. She was not, like them, risking her life on a dangerous impulse, but she began to understand how danger—any kind of danger—could hold a strange, addictive joy.

"Robyn?"

Emerging from her reflections, she turned her head to look at Shane. "Yes?" she responded, reaching up to brush back a strand of windblown hair and blinking at him in the still-hazy sunlight.

"Where did you get that?"

"What?"

"That suit you nearly have on."

"Why? Don't you like it?" she asked in injured innocence.

Shane very nearly glared at her. "If you're wearing it when we sail into Key West," he said flatly, ignoring her question, "you'll probably be arrested."

"Don't be ridiculous. Everything that should be covered is, so why worry?"

He looked as if he wanted to argue with her, but he said nothing more.

Robyn turned her face back up to the sun, feeling rewarded and wondering if her strategy was working as well as she hoped it was. She could feel Shane's eyes on her from time to time, and she discovered yet another unfamiliar sensation: a heady pleasure in the knowledge that he found her body beautiful. She felt a bit like an exhibitionist posing in her skimpy suit, but she told herself firmly that the cause was certainly worthwhile.

Shane's temper became more than a little frayed as the day wore on. He anchored the boat close to one of the small keys near Marathon at lunchtime and dove over the side without explanation. Robyn, whose suit really wasn't designed for swimming, calmly went below and fixed a lunch of sandwiches. A lunch Shane hardly did justice to when he emerged, dripping, from the sea.

Robyn kept her suit on until they got underway again, raising the sails herself this time. She was an old hand at it by now and didn't have to ask for instructions or help from her silently watching skipper.

Tying off the last sail, she started back toward Shane, wondering if she had imagined his low groan moments before. He certainly looked a bit odd, she thought, and she suffered a brief moment of compunction. But only a brief moment.

She wasn't *doing* anything, after all.

Robyn went down to her cabin and stared at herself for a long moment in the small mirror over the chests.

She carefully brushed the tangles from her hair, then
changed out of the suit and into a pair of very brief
white shorts and a flimsy button-down shirt, the tails
of which she tied in a knot beneath her breasts. No
bra, and it was obvious. She stared into the mirror
again, then turned away, muttering to herself, "I must
make a lousy vamp."

The afternoon, however, progressed quite nicely—
for her, anyway. Other sailboats were in strong evi-
dence as they neared Key West, and Robyn enjoyed
waving at anybody who waved at her. Most of the
wavers, she noted, were men. Shane didn't seem to
notice all the attention Robyn was drawing, but he
did swear somewhat violently when one busily waving
skipper nearly plowed his small sailboat into an even
smaller catamaran.

"You," Shane declared flatly, "ought to be locked
up!"

"Why?" She looked at him innocently.

"You're a hazard to navigation. And get that damned
cat down off the sail!"

"Temper, temper," she chided as she hurried to foil
George's attempt to see the world from the top of a
mast.

Prudently, she held George in her lap during the
rest of the trip into Key West. Nudging Shane was
one thing, she decided, but there was no sense in
shoving him. Coping with George was the straw he
didn't need. There was a fine line between passion
and anger.

They tied up the boat at a marina in Key West and
went ashore for the few remaining hours of daylight.
Shane kept Robyn close to his side while they visited
the lighthouse, the Aquarium, and the Little White
House. Drawing the inevitable masculine glances, Ro-

byn looked up once to see Shane bestow a stony glare on one perfectly harmless-looking man. She hid a satisfied smile.

She wondered vaguely if falling in love with Shane had done this to her: made her a mass of contradictory impulses. She wanted him, but didn't want to make a commitment. She had been grateful for his platonic rules only days before, but now she wanted them broken.

She wanted him to carry her off to their boat and make love to her until she couldn't think straight, until questions of right and wrong and what was good for her no longer mattered.

Lying alone, but for George, on her bunk that night, Robyn suspected a little grimly that Shane had finally caught on to her game. She wondered what had taken him so long. Not that it mattered. He knew now; there had been speculation in his eyes as he'd wished her good night up on deck. Now that there were two in the game, what role would he play?

He had become a little thoughtful while they'd eaten supper at a hamburger place, narrowed eyes watching her intently. But he had continued to talk to her casually, certainly not demanding an explanation for her behavior.

He didn't ask for an explanation on Saturday, either.

Robyn wore a skimpy bikini during the morning, waving energetically at other boats as they left the marina and nearly hanging over the side in her enthusiasm.

Shane looked amused.

Robyn dug out her bottle of suntan lotion once they were well underway, and asked him to get her back for her since she couldn't reach it.

Shane complied with perfect calm.

Robyn found the remains of the first day's bottle of wine and toasted his health all through lunch.

Shane drank half the bottle and stayed sober as a judge while Robyn fell asleep on the padded bench.

Robyn woke up mid-afternoon, feeling cranky, and purposely let George finally succeed in climbing to the top of the mast.

Shane laughed.

By the time they dropped anchor off Long Key late that afternoon, Robyn was ready to consign man and cat to Davey Jones's Locker and sail home alone.

Banging pots and pans in the galley while Shane got everything ready for night, she was torn between irritation and amusement. Some vamp she was! She couldn't even get the man drunk and take advantage of him, for God's sake!

Damn that chameleon she'd idiotically fallen in love with! She needed a scorecard to keep up with his moods. Wonderfully tender on that first night; utterly stricken when she'd told him about Brian; calm and reasonable when he'd proposed this trip; charming the first couple of days; bad-tempered and brooding yesterday; and completely cheerful today.

It'd serve him right, she thought sulkily, if she made him fix his own damn supper!

Before she could do more than roughly plan a meal, Shane was yelling down at her from the deck, effectively wiping rebellious thoughts away.

"Better make it a cold supper, Robyn!"

Robyn braced herself automatically as the gentle rocking motion of the boat began to increase in intensity. Frowning, she stared out the tiny porthole above the sink, uneasily realizing that the setting sun was now hidden behind leaden clouds. She quickly put away the pots and pans, hanging on to the sink from time to time to brace herself.

Latching everything securely, she started up the steps to the deck, meeting a nervous George and watching him over her shoulder as he dashed into her cabin.

She found Shane carefully tying the sails down, and her uneasiness increased as she saw his serious face. "What's going on?" she asked, looking worriedly at the choppy water surrounding them.

"Storm," he replied briefly, double-checking the knot he'd just tied. "Coming out of the Gulf."

"How bad?"

Shane must have heard the anxiety in her voice, because he turned his head to smile reassuringly at her. "Shouldn't be too bad. These late afternoon storms usually blow over pretty quickly. And we're in the lee of the island, which helps. We'll probably feel quite a bit of motion, though, so if you're nervous, you'd better go take a pill."

"I've been all right so far," she defended hesitantly.

"Suit yourself." He shrugged.

Robyn decided to take a motion-sickness pill just to be safe.

She'd nearly reached the steps when Shane called out to her.

"Have you started supper yet?"

"No." She paused, looking inquiringly at him.

"Just as well. We probably won't feel like eating until this is over with."

Having completely abandoned her attempts in the art of vamping, Robyn silently went below and took a pill. Two, actually. Then she sat on the narrow bench by the table in the galley and stared at the porthole. It darkened rapidly, brightened from time to time by flashes of lightning. Thunder rumbled distantly, and then closer.

Robyn became aware of rain pattering on the deck above her head just as she heard Shane's feet on the steps. A moment later, he was sliding onto the bench beside her.

"That should do it," he said as if to himself, then sent a sidelong glance at her tense face. "Not worried, are you?"

"Me? Worried? Why should I be worried?"

"We'll be fine, Robyn."

"Right," she murmured. "Right, skipper."

"I promise."

"I'll hold you to that."

Shane smiled slightly and then suddenly asked for his explanation. "Mind telling me the rules for the little game you've been playing since yesterday?"

Robyn stared at him for a long moment, then asked wryly, "Is this what's known as 'getting her mind off things'?"

"Acquit me of any ulterior motives. I'm just curious, that's all."

Suddenly embarrassed by his perception and her own ridiculous games, Robyn stared down at the table top, flushing. "Well, find something else to be curious about, dammit," she mumbled.

In a thoughtful voice, for all the world as though he were talking about something inconsequential, Shane said, "I couldn't decide whether to take you up on your somewhat blatant offer, or throw you overboard."

"Thanks!" she snapped tartly.

"However, since I'd already decided to abide by my good intentions, there was only one thing to do."

Robyn gave him a speaking glare. "Which was?"

"Enjoy the show," he stated solemnly.

She decided very sanely that the first chance she

got, she was going to brain him. Or hang him from the mast like a flag. Or—what was it?—keelhaul him. Or feed him to the sharks.

"So it was funny, huh?" she asked mildly.

"Not funny. Amusing."

"Some difference."

"A distinction, actually. A small distinction."

"Did you ever read that story 'Murder on the Boat'?"

"No." His lips were twitching.

"Stick around," she gritted.

The emerald eyes gleamed at her. "Actually, you make a pretty fair seductress," he commended judiciously.

Robyn's sense of humor suddenly began producing giggles. "Really? Then tell me, O knowing judge—what was wrong with my technique?"

"Wrong?" he asked innocently.

She watched as he rose from the bench and stepped over to the stove, expertly keeping his balance as he began to make a pot of coffee. "Yes, wrong. Obviously, I did something wrong."

"Well, there's one thing you didn't realize," he drawled, keeping one hand on the pot's handle as he held it over the burner.

"Which was?"

"All you had to do was ask," he explained gravely.

Robyn stared at him a bit wildly, totally oblivious now to the rocking of the boat.

"Coffee, Robyn? I think it's going to be a long night."

"You can say that again," she muttered.

CHAPTER
Seven

As the night wore on, Robyn drank black coffee steadily, watched lightning flash outside the porthole, and listened to the heavy rain and booming thunder. The rough motion of the boat didn't bother her, but she didn't try to get up from the bench to test her sea legs.

She was obstinately determined not to ask Shane to explain his cute little remark.

Shane seemed content to sit in silence, occasionally getting up to fill their cups or make more coffee.

By the time midnight crept by, with the storm still raging outside, Robyn was too sleepy to care much about anything except her inviting bunk in the cabin across the hall. Making a fool of oneself, she decided wryly, was certainly tiring.

With a certain perverse pleasure, she jabbed Shane

in the ribs with her elbow, and murmured, "Move, will you, please? You have to get out before I can, and I'm going to bed."

Shane slid out from the bench and got to his feet, rubbing his lean ribs and staring at her ruefully.

Robyn held on to the table until she found her balance, then looked up at him. "Since you obviously can't sleep on deck tonight, you're welcome to the other bunk."

"I can sleep in here."

She stared rather pointedly at his six-foot length and then at the miniscule floor space. "*George* couldn't stretch out in here, let alone you. Take the other bunk. I only hope you don't snore."

"You couldn't hear it even if I did," Shane retorted as another crash of thunder rattled the boat.

Not finding the remark worthy of response, Robyn carefully made her way out of the galley and into the cabin, grabbing an occasional doorframe or wall for support. Trusting that Shane would give her time enough to get ready for bed, she closed the cabin door, flipped on the light, and rapidly encountered problems.

For instance, it was damnably hard to balance on one foot with a boat heaving underneath that foot. And pulling off the knit top she had changed into after her nap gave her a giddy sense of vertigo and caused her to sit down rather abruptly on the floor.

Changing took much longer than usual, so that when Shane tapped on the door, she was just pulling her sleeping gear—a large white T-shirt—into place. "Come in," she muttered, her back to the door while she tried to pull her hair out from under the shirt.

"Need some help?" Shane asked in amusement when he opened the door and stepped into the cabin.

"Never." Robyn wasn't particularly in charity with

him at the moment, and didn't care if he knew it. Having finally won the wrestling match with her hair, she picked up her brush from the chest she was hanging on to and then stepped rather carefully over to the bottom bunk. Pushing George off her pillow, she crawled under the light blanket, still pointedly ignoring Shane.

There was barely room enough for her to sit up without banging her head on the top bunk, so she had to bend her neck a little. Brushing her long hair steadily, she murmured vaguely, "Get the light, will you?"

Leaning against the chest containing his clothes, Shane sighed. "Are you going to sulk all night?" he asked dryly.

"Probably," she reflected calmly, shooting him a guarded glance from the corner of her eyes. "By tomorrow, though, I'll probably be good and mad. Are you going to get the light?"

"In a minute. I think I should explain something first."

"Don't go to any trouble on my account," she advised politely.

He sighed again. "Robyn, before you waste a lot of energy getting mad at me—"

"I thought you wanted me to get mad. You told me not to be afraid to get mad at you."

"I meant for a good reason. This isn't."

"Funny, I thought it was."

"Dammit, are you going to listen to me?"

Robyn tossed her brush to the bottom of the bunk beside George, plumped up her pillow, and lay back. "What choice do I have? I can't walk on water, either."

Shane rested his weight on the low chest while he pulled off his sneakers, tossing them into a corner before beginning to unbutton his short-sleeved shirt.

"I thought you might be curious," he said casually, "to know why I've apparently been cutting off my nose to spite my face these last few days."

Robyn linked her fingers together behind her neck and stared fixedly at the underside of the top bunk. "So you're going to enlighten me?" she asked just as casually, but with her entire attention riveted on him.

"I think it's time." The light went out, and Shane climbed easily into the top bunk, murmuring, "Some things are better said in the dark. Especially when they're being said to an indignant lady."

"Don't bother being polite. Actually, I'm mad as hell."

He chuckled softly above her. "I know. That's why I want to lay all my cards on the table and be completely honest."

Robyn felt more than a little nervous when he said that, but her voice was calm when she responded, "Shane, if this trip has showed you that you really don't want to get involved with me, just say so."

"You know better than that. Robyn, when we met that night, I thought you were something I'd dreamed up. And after we'd spent the night together, I wouldn't have willingly let you go for any reason I could think of."

A peculiar hot-cold sensation churned in Robyn's middle at the seriousness of his deep voice, and she felt a fleeting sense of panic. The entire situation was about to come to a head, she knew, and she still wasn't ready to confess her fear... or her love.

Shane continued quietly, and even though they weren't touching and couldn't see each other, Robyn was aware of a strange, almost painful intimacy between them in the darkness.

"When I believed that you had a husband lurking around somewhere, I wasn't sure what I felt. Rage, jealousy, even betrayal. But stronger than anything else was the desire to see you again, to find out if you'd been struck by lightning that night the way I had."

"Lightning?" Her voice was barely a whisper.

"Didn't you feel it, too?" He sighed roughly. "Songs and poems are written about it, psychologists try to analyze it, scientists try to explain it logically, skeptics say it doesn't exist." He paused for a moment, then went on huskily, "I was never in that last group, honey; I always believed in love. But I never expected to look across a crowded room and fall head over heels in love with a tiny, raven-haired, golden-eyed mystery lady."

"Love at first sight?" she asked unsteadily, a part of her wanting to see his face for the truth, and yet already knowing that he was speaking it.

"Why do you think I've been chasing after you like a madman?" He swore softly, roughly, his voice half amused and half pained. "I wouldn't admit this to anyone except you, honey, but my dreams of romance were just that—dreams. Vague, impractical things. I never expected to have to deal with the memory of another man, or those fears of yours that are keeping us apart."

Robyn swallowed hard, her throat dry. "Fears?"

"We both know you're afraid. I was hoping this trip..." His voice trailed away, and he cleared his throat. "I don't know what you're afraid of, Robyn— whether something about your marriage has you afraid of a commitment, or whether it's me—"

"Not you," she interrupted quickly. "Never you."

"Well, that's something." He shifted restlessly in his bunk. "I hope you'll tell me what you're afraid of when you're ready to. All along, I've felt as though I were...fighting something in the dark. It seemed best to just take things one day at a time, to give you time to get to know me. I didn't think I was getting anywhere until you started your seduction act on Friday."

The amusement in that last sentence brought a flush to Robyn's face, but she was curious. "You knew . . . that I wanted you before that. You knew the first day on the boat. Why did yesterday make a difference?"

Shane answered slowly, as though he were working it out in his own mind. "The first couple of days on the boat, you were . . . aware of me. The electricity, or whatever it is, between us wouldn't let it be any other way. But you were still running scared. Then something changed. You admitted that you wanted to touch me, needed to, and instead of taking the decision out of your hands and making love to you, I told you that I wanted you to be sure."

He chuckled suddenly. "I'm just guessing, honey, but I think that's what made you mad. You stopped running long enough to turn around and fight. But you still wanted me to make the decision, so you started pushing me."

Listening, open-mouthed, in the bunk below, Robyn realized abruptly just how childishly she'd been acting. Shane was right, damn him! She'd wanted to be absolved of the responsibility, swept off her feet and able to make only a token protest.

"Are you psychic?" she mumbled.

"I'm right, then?"

"Bull's-eye."

His voice was warm with amusement. "That's when I realized I was getting someplace. Even though you didn't want to commit yourself, you still wanted me badly enough to be a bit reckless."

"Oh, God, I feel like a fool!" she moaned, grateful for the sheltering darkness.

"That wasn't my intention, honey," he murmured, his voice becoming serious. "But I wasn't kidding when I said you only had to ask. I'm not trying to punish you for anything, and I hope to God you don't think that! I just believe that you should be sure enough about what you want to throw away the games and face up to how you feel. When you tell me what you want, honey, I'll know that you're willing to take the first step toward commitment."

Robyn drew the blanket up around her shoulders, suddenly feeling chilled in the hot, stuffy room. "And what do you want, Shane?" she whispered.

Very quietly, he answered, "I want you to marry me, honey."

Panic ricocheted through her mind, leaving bruises and pain. "Shane, don't—"

"Ssshh," he interrupted soothingly. "I'm not trying to pressure you, Robyn. I'll wait as long as it takes. I just want you to know that I want you to be my wife more than anything in the world. And we'll take all the time you need to work out those fears of yours."

Robyn wanted very badly to touch him, her hand lifting almost instinctively toward his bunk and then falling back. She wanted him to hold her and reassure her and tell her everything would be all right. But she knew that, once in his arms, sanity would vanish...and he wanted her to know exactly what she was doing.

"We only met a week ago," she murmured finally, trying to be rational, reasonable. "How can you be so sure that—that you want to marry me?"

"I'm sure." His voice was very certain. "I've been looking for you all my life, Robyn. I think you've lived in my dreams for years. And I'll walk barefoot through hell to keep you."

After a moment, he continued softly, "I've waited too long for you to lose you by impatience, honey. Now, we'd better get some sleep. We have a long day ahead of us tomorrow. Good night."

"Good night," she whispered, her mind on everything but sleep. She lay awake for a long time, staring at the underside of Shane's bunk, her thoughts, dreams, and desires confused and uncertain.

Her last clear thought before sleep ruthlessly claimed her weary mind was the vague realization that Shane had chosen to tell her of his love in the darkness because he believed that she was unable, or unwilling, to return that love.

Hours later, she woke with chilling suddenness, her hand lifting to cover her mouth and muffle the cry that would have disturbed Shane. She found herself curled into a tight ball on the bunk, her heart thudding painfully, the nightmare as vivid as though it were still replaying before her eyes.

The cabin was hot, stuffy, and suddenly stifling, and she had to have fresh air. Carefully, she straightened her cramped limbs and eased herself from the bunk. Only dimly aware that the boat was almost motionless, the storm over, she crossed the cabin to the open door, closing it behind her softly.

Wearing only the T-shirt, Robyn climbed the steps in darkness, knowing her way instinctively by now. The light, cool breeze on the deck was a blessing, and she knelt beside the padded bench, resting her elbows on the vinyl covering.

She stared out over the water, her gaze fixed on the still-blackened eastern horizon. Her nightmare hovered like a relentless nemesis, demanding to be seen, to be faced.

She bit her lip, her mind's eye re-creating the nightmare, just as it had really happened on the small television screen she had watched dumbly. Brian's crash. The twisted, flaming wreckage held in cruel focus by the camera. Firemen and paramedics...

And then the scene changed, and her most recent nightmare began, hurting her as nothing had before. Now it was Shane's broken, charred body they were pulling from the blackened metal death trap.

Tears rolled down Robyn's cheeks, hot and silent, and she tasted the coppery blood from her bitten lip. That cruel, heartbreaking vision would remain with her, she knew, as long as Shane raced. Eating away at her strength, her courage. Destroying her.

Once committed, she would cling to him as she had never clung to Brian, try in a hundred small ways to keep him by her side. Cut off his freedom. Smother him.

No. No, she couldn't do that. She had to find out if she was strong enough to watch him leave her side and climb heedlessly into a cage of death. Because if she couldn't—if she didn't face and conquer that fear—she would always be afraid of something. Weak and helpless in the grip of uncontrollable terror.

It was right, she knew, to fear for Shane when he raced. That fear was rational and understandable. But the terror she felt went far beyond anything rational. And it didn't stop at racing. She was terrified of losing Shane...in *any* way.

It wasn't possible to chain him to her side for fear of losing him. It was the quickest, surest way she knew of to destroy love, and two lives as well. And asking him to give up racing would be—if he agreed to—the first link in that deadly chain.

If only she weren't so afraid. If only the vision of Brian's death didn't keep haunting her. And her father's death in yet another twisted wreck only three years ago . . .

Robyn rested her head on her folded arms, letting the tears flow freely at last. She felt as if she were at the end of her rope, and she wasn't even sure she possessed the courage to face Shane.

When she finally raised her head, the eastern sky had lightened to slate gray and her knees were numb from kneeling on the hard deck. She gazed around absently, then frowned and reached underneath the bench, finding the storage locker and the sleeping bag Shane kept there. She got to her feet stiffly, automatically unrolling and unzipping the bag and spreading it out on the deck.

Stepping to the middle of the quilted softness, she sank back down to her knees. Feet beneath her, she folded her hands limply on her bare thighs and faced east. Like some brooding Buddha, she waited patiently for the sun.

It had been a long time since Robyn had watched a sunrise. It had been a favorite pastime of her childhood, but the wonder of those precious moments had somehow gotten lost during her adult years of change and turmoil.

Now a peculiar sense of peace stole over her, bestowed by the peace all around her. No sound disturbed the new day; even the sea was still. Only the gentle lapping of water against the side of the boat was audible, and the soft steady sound was as comforting as a heartbeat. Robyn thought dimly that the problems of the world disappeared in the beauty of a new dawn, and she felt her own fears and worries gradually fade away.

The horizon had lightened to a deep blue, the last stars had gently winked out overhead, and Robyn was acutely aware that she was no longer alone. As though he were an extension of herself, she felt Shane kneel behind her on the sleeping bag. Her mind curiously suspended, she wondered if he had come because she had wanted him here, because the moment needed him to be complete.

He slipped his arms around her silently, fitting her within the warm hollow of his thighs, his hands covering hers. Robyn leaned her head back against his shoulder, barely breathing as she watched the new day being born. That Shane shared her fascination, she knew; his body was utterly still, his eyes fixed on the horizon, his breath gently stirring her hair. And she could feel his heart beating steadily, keeping time with the lapping water.

Blue lightened to violet and then to pink as the sun announced its coming—hesitating now, teasing them with the delay. Then the first crescent of orange topped the horizon, and shafts of light began to coat the sea in silver. It seemed to hesitate yet again, and Robyn held her breath, almost certain that Shane did the same.

The huge orange ball rose slowly, majestically, like a king rising before an audience of rapt subjects. Robyn felt her lips curving into a smile, certain that this birth was more beautiful than yesterday's.

"So beautiful," she whispered. "So perfect."

Shane's arms tightened around her, and his voice was as hushed as hers when he murmured, "The touch of dawn washes everything clean and new."

Watching the sun rising, its orange brightening to yellow, Robyn felt Shane's statement sinking into her mind, taking hold, giving her the new perspective she had needed so badly.

She half turned in his embrace, still resting between his warm thighs as she stared up at him. "A new beginning," she whispered, her voice filling with wonder. "A fresh start."

Shane smiled down at her, his emerald eyes shining with the love he had admitted last night. One large hand lifted to cup her cheek. With the perception that astonished and exhilarated her, he murmured softly, "A new beginning for the world...or for us?"

Speaking as much to herself as to him, she whispered, "I've been afraid to take that first step—to move forward or back. But every day begins new. You said it yourself. The touch of dawn washes everything clean. Every *day* is a fresh start."

Shane's thumb brushed her bottom lip, and then his smile faded and his eyes dropped to the tiny wound he had found. "You've hurt yourself," he murmured, frowning.

"Not anymore." A smile trembled on her lips. "I'm not going to hurt myself anymore."

His gaze lifted swiftly to meet hers, the emerald eyes immediately darkening, becoming bottomless pools. "Robyn...?" he breathed questioningly.

"I'm asking, Shane," she whispered, her hands moving to touch his bare, hair-roughened chest. "Will you make love with me?"

His eyes flared suddenly, and if Robyn had possessed any doubts about his love for her, they were erased. Because she recognized that look. From the very beginning, his vivid eyes had flared with that half savage, half tender emotion, and she knew now that it was love. The fierce yet gentle love she had wanted for so long...

And Robyn was taking her first step by dawn's light.

Shane pulled her abruptly closer, nearly crushing

her against his broad chest, his mouth finding hers in desperate need. Robyn locked her arms around him, her desire rising in a flaming fury to meet and clash with his.

She had never been so sure of anything in her life as she was that this moment was right. The sun was rising on a new day and . . . Yes. Yes!

Robyn felt his tongue exploring, possessing, and her own tongue joined the passionate game. Her nails lightly scratched the rippling muscles of his back, and she felt him shudder and draw her impossibly closer.

Shane's mouth left hers, dropping tender, burning kisses over her eyes, her nose, the hollows beneath her ears, her throat.

"What if the Coast Guard sails by?" she questioned throatily, only mildly interested.

"We'll wave at them," he answered hoarsely, intent on exploring the warm flesh of her throat.

Robyn laughed and then gasped as one of his hands slipped up beneath her shirt and closed over a breast. When he suddenly began pulling her shirt off, she helped, anxious to do away with the barriers separating them. Shane quickly removed his shorts, tossing them aside.

He drew her down to lie beside him on the quilted softness of the sleeping bag, emerald fires raking her slender, golden body. "God, but you're beautiful!" he groaned softly.

Her eyes, in their turn, were taking in the lean strength of his body. "So are you," she told him huskily, feeling the same wonder she had felt in a lamplit hotel room a lifetime ago.

The lion's growl rumbled from the depths of Shane's chest as he bent his head, his mouth hotly capturing the hardened tip of one aching breast. His tongue swirled maddeningly around the taut bud, seemingly insatiable in its hunger. His hands explored, fondled.

Robyn bit her lip with a moan when his fingers gently probed the quivering center of her, her body instinctively arching against his. His mouth transferred its attentions from one breast to the other, his fingers continuing their erotic caress.

Tension splintered through Robyn, and her nails dug into his shoulders as Shane's lips moved in a burning trail over the sensitive skin beneath her breasts, settling for a moment on her navel where his tongue dipped hotly, then moved lower.

Through half-opened eyes, Robyn watched the mast soaring above her head begin to spin drunkenly, feeling that she was in the middle of some wild cosmic storm. Dizzily closing her eyes, she felt the heat of the sun and of her desire, and she didn't know or care which was stronger.

"Shane!" It was half a protest, half a plea to continue his spellbinding touches.

"You're beautiful," he rasped, the feel of his words against her flesh nearly driving her crazy.

Robyn felt the excitement spiraling crazily, becoming a primitive, driving rush toward release. She was carried along helplessly on the wave, moaning raggedly, the hands she held him with going white with nearly unbearable tension. And then the world dissolved.

She floated for timeless moments, drained almost to the very depths of her soul.

She opened her eyes slowly as Shane came up to rest beside her, his body taut, his emerald fires blazing down at her. When he bent his head to kiss her gently, blotting out the sunlight, Robyn felt the fires within herself kindling to new life.

Pushing almost fiercely against his chest, she rolled

with him, coming to rest on top of him as the kiss ended. She felt a sudden yearning to know him as he knew her, to explore every inch of his body until it was as familiar as her own.

She pressed teasing kisses against his throat, his shoulders, her lips finding and capturing the flat male nipples. Concentrating only on pleasing him, she was barely aware of his hands unsteadily stroking her hair, her back. She slid her lips over his flat, hard belly and then lifted her head.

Slowly, almost hesitantly, she rested one hand on his chest while she explored with the other, feeling his heart hammering wildly. He jerked slightly as she touched him, held him, and his breath caught with a rasping sound in his throat.

Robyn caressed him gently, tentatively. And then she bent her head once again, her long hair forming a curtain around her face as she tasted every inch of his flesh she could reach. She felt no shame, no hesitation now. With a need beyond reason, she had to know him.

"Robyn!" he groaned hoarsely, and then she was being lifted and turned as easily as a child. She felt the softness of the sleeping bag beneath her back. Shane rose above her, the emerald fires now burning almost out of control.

She felt his weight, welcomed him eagerly, and as they became as close as separate beings could ever be, looked deeply into his eyes. There she saw undisguised love burning even brighter than desire.

In that timeless moment, Robyn became acutely aware of his stark vulnerability, and his willingness to show her that. That realization crumbled her last defense. Locking her arms around his neck, she cried huskily, "I love you, Shane! I love you."

Shane went still for a moment, something very fierce and male flashing in his eyes. He lowered his head, kissing her with that tender, savage passion she loved. "Robyn...beautiful Robyn...I love you so much!"

They began to move together with the grace of trained dancers, each of them giving and taking until they were drained and filled and drained again. Like helpless voyagers adrift in the heart of a raging sea, they clung to one another as the only stable things in a universe gone mad.

And then even that crazy universe turned inside out, and they crashed to shore like shooting stars.

Robyn was the first to stir from the limp, exhausted tangle of arms and legs, and then it was only because she felt the sun beating down on her and was suddenly worried about being sunburned in uncomfortable places.

"Do you always seduce your women on the high seas?" she asked in a muffled voice, trying to move and finding very little energy for it.

"Never," Shane responded in a lazy voice. "You did the seducing."

"I did not," she objected, managing at last to raise her head and stare down at him. "I was a total washout as a vamp. You told me so."

"Not a *total* washout." Shane didn't bother to open his eyes. "With a little practice, you'll be topnotch. I'll let you practice on me. S'matter of fact, I won't mind a bit."

"That's big of you." With an effort, Robyn disentangled herself and sat up. She found herself staring at a little island off their port side, and she suddenly had a horrible thought. "Shane, does anybody live on that island?"

"Key. And I wouldn't be a bit surprised." He opened

one eye and peered at her. "Why? Worried about your modesty?"

She transferred her gaze to him, not greatly surprised to find that she felt no shyness. Not with him. From the very beginning, she'd been without modesty with him. "Well, it's a little late for that," she pointed out wryly. "But shouldn't we shove off before somebody calls the police?"

With startling energy, Shane rose to his feet and lifted her easily in his arms. "No. First, we're going for a swim. Then we'll have breakfast. We'll get around to shoving off later." He smiled down at her, apparently not the least bit concerned that if there was a watcher on the Key, he was getting an eyeful.

In the same calm voice, he demanded, "Now tell me, beautiful witch—did I really hear what I thought I heard in that dream I just had?"

Robyn stared at him for a moment, then smiled slowly. "I hope you heard it. A woman likes to be heard when she tells a man she loves him."

Shane's eyes held a trace of wonder. "And a man likes to be loved by the woman he loves," he said huskily. His arms tightened around her. "I wasn't sure we'd make it, sweetheart."

Her smile faltered for just a second. "There are still some . . . rough seas ahead," she warned lightly.

"I know." The deep voice was sober. "You'll tell me all about it when you're ready."

And with the abruptness of his earlier movements, he threw her overboard. Robyn came up sputtering. Treading water and pushing her hair out of her eyes, she glared up at him. "That was a rotten, no-good, low-down, sneaky trick!" she yelled at him.

"How's the water, honey?" Shane asked with interest, evidently completely unabashed by his nakedness or his actions as he leaned over the side.

"I'll get you for this!"

"Is that a promise?" He leered, arching his eyebrows.

"Dammit, this water's cold!"

"A brisk, reviving swim—that's what we both need."

"*We?* I don't see you out here. What's that over there? Is that a shark?" she yelped.

"No, it's a stick in the water."

"I saw it move!"

"The current made it twitch. Stop imagining things."

"You're a funny man." Robyn splashed water toward him, irritated when her aim fell short. "Well? Are you going to stand there and smirk all morning, or are you going to join me in the cradle of the deep?"

Shane grinned at her. "Having a lively sense of self-preservation, I have no intention of coming in until I'm reasonably sure you won't try to drown me."

"Who, me?" Robyn smiled innocently. "Why worry? You're bigger than I am."

"Yes, but you're a witch, and witches cast spells and things. Eye of newt and toe of bat and so on."

Robyn laughed so hard she nearly forgot to tread water. "Bats don't have toes!"

"Whatever." He raised one foot to rest on the chrome railing and leaned an elbow on his knee. "Anyway, I don't want you casting any more spells. I'm still tangled up in the first one."

"The first one?"

"Sure. I looked across a room and tumbled into a pair of golden eyes. Definitely a spell." His emerald eyes were acquiring a gleam she recognized well.

Robyn eyed him carefully. "You seem to have recovered rather quickly from your exhaustion," she observed.

"You noticed that, huh?"

"It's a little difficult not to."

"Mermaids in the water do that to me." He smiled slowly. "One sure difference between a man and a woman...a man can't hide his desire."

"Especially a naked man," she pointed out.

"Are you complaining?"

Robyn took another stab at the art of vamping. Smiling gently, she murmured, "I'm simply wondering why you're still on the boat..."

She read the intent, flaring expression in his eyes long before he left the boat in a clean dive, and she hastily began swimming away. He caught her before she'd taken three strokes.

"Come here, witch..."

"Shane? Shane, not in the water! We'll drown!"

CHAPTER
Eight

THEY DIDN'T MAKE very good time that day, which was—as Robyn gleefully pointed out more than once—all Shane's fault. Periodically, he would suddenly drop the sails, allowing the boat to drift, and lunge at Robyn. And since she couldn't run very far on a boat, he inevitably caught her.

"I've spent half the day trying to keep my clothes on!"

"I didn't notice you trying very hard a few minutes ago."

"A gentleman wouldn't point that out."

"Gentlemen don't have any fun."

The boat nearly ran aground on a sandbar once while they were otherwise occupied, and then later showed a tendency to drift toward the Bahamas. After that, Shane began dropping the anchor when he dropped the sails.

George climbed the mast and sails from time to time, then apparently lost interest in the game when neither of his human companions objected. He sulked on Robyn's bunk for the rest of the day.

Robyn had never been happier in her life. She was delighted by the fact that Shane couldn't let brief moments go by without touching her and holding her— delighted because she felt the same way about him. Laughter and teasing and love surrounded her, claimed her, and she pushed the fears from her mind. Like Scarlett O'Hara, she would think about that tomorrow.

Since Shane *said* he was determined that they reach Key Largo by sundown, they didn't stop the boat for lunch. Robyn went below and made sandwiches, bringing everything up on deck and feeding Shane a bite at a time while he steered.

"You know, I really don't know much about you," she commented thoughtfully a little while later, sitting cross-legged on the bench in one of Shane's shirts. "Generalities, but no specifics."

"What do you want to know?" Shane was spending more time gazing at her with glowing eyes than paying attention to their course.

"Well, everything, obviously! Tell me about your family...and where you live when you're not traveling...and your favorite colors...and what you plan to do with your life...Good Lord—I don't know *anything* about you!"

He chuckled softly. "We can fix that. Let's see— my family. I think I told you that Mother runs the family wine business. My father died about ten years ago. I have three younger sisters, two of them married and one still in college." He slanted Robyn a grin. "I spent a lot of years playing big brother. And they all still run to me when they have a problem, which I'm glad of."

The brief sketch told Robyn more, perhaps, than Shane knew. It told her that he was accustomed to responsibilities, which he didn't shirk. Inevitably, she compared him to Brian, whose recklessness had carried over into his personal life. He had always left responsibility to others.

Shane was chuckling again. "Sharon, the youngest, is suffering the pangs of love at the moment. Or she was when she called me a couple of weeks ago. She's after some med student at UCLA, and since she's majoring in history, they don't seem to have much in common."

Robyn smiled at him. "So she called big brother for advice. And what did big brother tell her?"

"To keep looking! My baby sister has fallen in love a dozen times in the last year alone. I keep telling her not to try so hard."

Laughing, Robyn observed, "I bet she liked that!"

"Sure." Shane grimaced slightly. "I've heard cleaner language from liberty-bound sailors."

Robyn smiled at the affection in his voice, then prodded curiously. "Do you all live in California? When you're not traveling, I mean?"

"As a matter of fact, aside from Sharon, who comes home for holidays, we all live within a few miles of each other. The business is in the northern end of Napa Valley. Mother lives nearest to it. My oldest sister, Connie, married a lawyer, and they live nearby. Beth's the middle sister. She startled all of us a few years ago by marrying the eldest son of a vintner— our biggest rival! I don't know who was more dismayed, Mother or Beth's new father-in-law."

"Montague and Capulet?" Robyn teased, her lips twitching.

"Only in tragedies!" Shane laughed softly. "Actually, Mother and Alan's father accepted the situation with good grace. The rivalry is a cordial one."

"A missed opportunity!" Robyn mourned with mock regret. "Just think how romantic it would have been: a modern day story of star-crossed lovers! A family feud—"

Shane grinned at her. "No way! For one thing, Beth's no weeping Juliet. She would have told us all to go to hell and marched off with Alan to conquer a world or two. And I'm sure Alan could slay dragons with the best of them."

"Really?" Robyn lifted an inquiring brow. "And how are you at slaying dragons? A woman likes to know these things."

"Not bad." Shane pursed his lips thoughtfully. "Although I think I'm better at scaring away things that go bump in the night."

"Dragons don't go bump?"

"Have you ever *seen* a dragon? They're huge. Absolutely huge. Before you hear the bump, you're squashed flat."

"Then how do you slay them?"

"Where on earth did you go to school? I've never heard such ignorance! Dragons are slain with magic swords, of course."

"I beg your pardon," Robyn sputtered, biting the inside of her lip to keep from laughing out loud. "I thought it was slingshots."

"That was Goliath," Shane informed her pityingly.

"Oh." She reflected for a moment. "Are there dragons in Napa Valley? Do they squash the grapes?"

"Oh, we drove them deep into the mountains years ago," he told her loftily. With spur-of-the-moment invention, he continued gravely, "They only come out in years ending in a zero, and then we find a witch to curse them until they hide again."

"I *knew* you had an ulterior motive!" she accused.

"Of course. I need a resident witch. With her own familiar and a book of spells to keep the dragons away, so I won't have to dent my magic sword."

"Oh, damn," she murmured mournfully. "And I traded my book of spells to a wizard for stardust! I'm afraid you'll just have to keep looking for your witch. I won't do at all."

"Are you kidding? It took me too long to find you. We just won't tell the dragons about the book. You can chant at them in pig Latin or something. They'll never know the difference."

"I'd never have the nerve. Dragons terrify me."

"Nonsense. I'd be standing by with my magic sword, just in case."

Robyn's laughter finally began escaping. "Oh, God!" she gasped. "I've never been party to such a ridiculous conversation in my life!"

Shane grinned at her, but then the grin faded, replaced by a frown. "Hey, witch-lady," he ordered, "get your butt over here."

"I *beg* your pardon!" Her voice was frosty, but she relented beneath his narrow-eyed, threatening stare and got her butt over there. "I'm here, skipper," she said meekly, but with a grin.

Shane hauled her against his side with one arm, resting his chin on the top of her head. "It's been nearly half an hour since I've touched you," he complained gruffly. "I was beginning to suffer withdrawal symptoms."

Robyn slipped her arms around his waist, rubbing her cheek against his bare chest with kittenlike contentment. "You never told me where you live in Napa Valley," she murmured.

"Actually, I live above the valley. I have a house halfway up a mountain. Lots of wood and stone, and huge windows with a terrific view. It stands empty for most of the year, now, but I'm hoping that'll soon change. Would you like to live in a mountain aerie, witch-lady?"

The casual question demanded a casual answer, and Robyn swallowed hard before she could supply one. "I think... that I'd love to live in a mountain aerie," she finally got out lightly. "As long as my dragonslayer lived there, too."

He brushed his lips against her forehead gently. "Your dragonslayer," he vowed huskily, "will always be there. He'd sell his soul to the devil for a promise of eternity with you, love."

Robyn shut her eyes against the bright reflection of sunlight off the water and refused to let herself think about eternity. Or even tomorrow. "I love you, Shane," she whispered.

"I love you, too, honey. So very much."

They stood that way for a long time, only the snapping of wind in the sails and the splash of water disturbing the peace of their surroundings. Then Shane—perhaps sensing, with his uncanny perception, her need to hold the fears at bay with laughter—became playful once again.

His hand slid downward and shaped a rounded hip. In a shocked voice, he exclaimed, "My God—the woman's wearing nothing but this flimsy shirt! Are you lost to all decency?"

Robyn batted his hand away and laughed. "You should know. I seem to remember express orders from the skipper to wear something without snaps, buttons, or zippers. That was after my shorts and top bit the dust for the third time."

"Counting your conquests—and at your age, too!"

"I'm putting notches on my belt." She gasped suddenly as his hand returned to probe more intimately beneath the shirt. "What *are* you doing?" she asked breathlessly.

"Well, if you don't know by now—"

"Shane! Look, there's another boat coming! They'll call the Coast Guard, and we'll be arrested for shocking the fish or something. Darling, put both hands on the wheel—!"

The "darling" was nearly her undoing, since Shane promptly showed signs of abandoning the wheel and shocking more than the fish. She somehow managed, however, to be sitting decorously on the padded bench when the other boat sailed by. Fortunately, she reflected, the other skipper and crew weren't close enough to observe her flush or the gleam in Shane's eyes.

In spite of everything, they reached Key Largo by the time the sun was setting. But Robyn was somewhat puzzled at first when Shane decided that they would drop anchor in a small cove rather than enter the marina they had stopped at before.

"No marina?" she questioned.

"I don't think so."

"Why not?"

"Well, those bunks below are pretty narrow."

Light dawned, but Robyn kept a straight face. "So?"

"We'll be up here on deck." Busily tying one of the sails, he slanted a gleaming look her way. "And it's remotely possible that we could shock narrow-minded neighbors in the marina."

Solemnly, Robyn said, "We wouldn't want to do that."

"Of course not."

"You're a dirty old man."

"I am not old!" Shane protested indignantly.

"You have a one-track mind."

"Quoth the vamp."

"*I* didn't nearly run us aground. And I didn't let the boat drift toward Cuba, either."

"Of course not. And you didn't look at me with bedroom eyes all day. Or call me darling and distract me all to hell."

"Well, if you don't like it—"

"I like it too much, witch, and you know it! But if you don't help me tie down these sails, I may not be a nice guy and let you out of galley duty tonight the way I'd planned."

Robyn promptly went to help him. "I don't have to cook? What did you have in mind? No, don't answer that. I *know* what you have in mind!" She dodged his playfully threatening hand and continued teasingly, "But neither man nor woman lives by shocking the fishes alone. We have to eat."

"We'll shock the fishes *after* we eat. If you ask me nicely, I just might let you watch the master chef at work."

"Doing what?"

"What master chefs do best. Grab that line, will you?"

"I will if you'll stop grabbing me!"

"I like grabbing you."

"Really? I never would have guessed if you hadn't told me. *Now* look what you've done! I only have three buttons left on this shirt, dammit."

"Your vamping abilities are coming along nicely."

"Shane!"

The night passed in a dreamy haze as far as Robyn was concerned. Making love under the stars was an experience she would treasure for the rest of her life, and Shane's tenderness seemed to deepen and grow with every passing hour. He made no attempt to hide the awe he felt at the incredible feelings between them, and his openness sparked an openness in Robyn that she hadn't known she possessed.

But "tomorrow" inevitably came, and all too soon they were beginning the last leg of their trip only miles out of Miami. The morning slipped past quickly, filled with the laughter and teasing that made Robyn feel as if she'd known Shane for years.

"I feel like the sultan's favorite girl," she grumbled once. "Will you *stop* looking at me like that?"

"Like what?" He was smiling.

"Like you're the sultan!"

"Your lord and master, in fact."

"Gloria Steinem freed the slaves."

"Well, she missed one." He ducked hastily. "Witch! You just threw a perfectly good shoe overboard, and I'm not going back for it!"

"That's all right. It was your shoe."

After Shane had wreaked awful vengeance on his unrepentant crew, they got back underway and, since the wind held, rapidly made up for lost time. By the middle of the afternoon, they were almost within shouting distance of Miami.

Robyn fell silent as they neared their destination, feeling fear take hold of her and this time refuse to be shaken loose or pushed away. Shane would race in exactly one week, and she didn't know if she would have the strength to face it.

She had to tell him about Brian's death and her fear of racing. Knowing Shane as she did now, she had no doubts that he would instantly offer to stop racing. And, though that was exactly what Robyn wanted him to do, she couldn't allow it. She had to conquer her unreasonable terror before it spread to other areas of her life and destroyed her. She would not be a coward.

"Robyn."

She looked up quickly from her seat on the bench and saw that Shane was watching her steadily. He held out a hand, and she went to him immediately, sliding her arms around his waist as he drew her close to his side.

"You're nerving yourself up to tell me, aren't you?" he asked quietly, rubbing his chin slowly against her forehead.

Robyn nodded once, listening to the comforting beat of his heart and wishing they could just sail away somewhere and abandon the world.

"We'll work it out, honey." His voice was steady, firm. "We'll take all the time you need and work it out. Whatever it is."

"I know." She held on to the solidness of his body as if it were a life line. "I know we will." But time, Robyn knew, had nearly run out. If she could face this upcoming race, she could face the rest. And if she couldn't . . . then no amount of time would help her.

Some time later, they worked together silently tying up the boat in the marina. Then they spent two hours cleaning and leaving everything just as they'd found it. Shane took care of getting rid of the perishable foodstuffs while Robyn neatened the galley and the bathroom. Finally, they gathered their things together and left the boat, Robyn carrying George securely in her arms.

The black Porsche was waiting where they'd left it, and within moments they were on their way to Robyn's house.

She had been aware for some time of the anxiety in Shane's eyes when he looked at her, but she could find no way to reassure him. Thinking of a sunrise and of new beginnings, she watched the sun as it began to lower itself in the western sky.

By the time Shane stopped the Porsche in front of the house, Robyn was strangely calm, ready to rid herself of her last burden of truth. It was time to take the next step.

Shane got her duffel bag out of the car and followed her up the walkway, not pressing for the answers he must have sensed were soon to come.

Marty opened the door just as they reached it, her eyes lighting up when she saw Robyn. The intent glance swept from top to toe, taking in Robyn's golden tan, the neat shorts and knit top, and the quiet glow in her eyes. Then she looked thoughtfully at Shane, standing just behind Robyn with one hand resting almost protectively on her shoulder.

Apparently Marty drew her own conclusions from what she saw. "Welcome back," she said, including Shane in her smile and stepping back to let them come in.

"Hi, Marty." Robyn kissed her lightly on the cheek as she passed. "Back all safe and sound."

"So I see." Marty lifted a pointed eyebrow at the cat as she shut the door behind them. "And one more than when you left."

Robyn smiled down at the cat, and then at Marty. "This is our mascot, King George."

"The third," Shane added, setting the duffel bag down by the door.

"The third," Robyn affirmed. "Marty, would you please take him into the kitchen and find him something to eat? Shane and I have to talk for a while."

Marty didn't ask the obvious question of why they hadn't talked on their trip. She simply looked at Robyn for a moment and then calmly accepted the cat and headed for the kitchen.

Robyn turned and reached to grasp Shane's hand.

"There's something I want to show you," she said, managing a smile to ease the anxiety in his eyes.

"I love you, Robyn," he said huskily.

Staring up at him, she realized suddenly that his anxiety was mixed with real fear. A fear of *her* fear. He knew only that whatever it was, it was standing between them. And Robyn knew that he was worried about losing her.

She hadn't meant to build this moment of confession into what it had become: something tense and frightening to them both. Somehow, in that moment, his vulnerability sparked a strength and determination in her greater than she had ever known before.

"Shane," she said very quietly, "I've been looking for you all my life. There was a place in me that nobody saw, nobody touched—not even me. And then you came, and I was whole, alive, for the very first time. I won't give that up. I won't give you up."

He reached up to touch her cheek lightly with his free hand, and a sigh seemed to come from deep inside him. The emerald eyes flared with that fierce glow. "Show me what it is you're afraid of, love."

Silently, she led him to a closed door across from the den, opened it, and led him inside, closing the door behind them and flipping a switch to light several lamps in the room.

It was a large room, furnished as a formal living room. But the closed draperies and curiously empty scent marked it as a room seldom if ever used. It was a room for guests, for displaying one's pride away from the clutter of everyday life.

Robyn leaned back against the door and watched Shane, vaguely surprised that the room caused her no pain this time, no heartache. It was almost as if someone else's memories were stored here.

Shane stared slowly around the room, his green

eyes taking in the trophies, plaques, and medals. He stepped over to a low table, heavy with photographs, and picked up one framed in silver. It was of a man, smiling, triumphant, holding a huge silver cup. A dark-haired man, lean, handsome, with a devil-light of recklessness in his blue eyes.

In a low voice, Robyn said, "Brian's father comes here sometimes. I thought he might be hurt if all this stuff were packed away. So I've kept it in here. And kept the door closed."

Shane looked up to meet Robyn's steady gaze. "McAllaster," he murmured. "Brian McAllaster. He was your husband."

"Yes. And he was killed in one of those damned cars."

There was a dawning understanding in Shane's eyes as he replaced the photo and stepped toward her. "That's why you didn't want to get involved with me," he said slowly.

She nodded. "I swore to myself after Brian was killed that I'd never again get involved with a man who raced. And then I met you." She stared down at her clasped hands. "Kris told me the next day that you raced. So I . . . convinced myself that I had pretended you were Brian."

"You lied about that?"

The hope in his voice brought her head up again, and she smiled at him a little sadly. "I lied. First to myself, and then to you. I was terrified of loving another reckless man."

"Reckless? Honey—"

Robyn held up a hand to stop him. "Let me explain everything first, all right?" She waited for his nod and then moved over to the couch and sat down. When Shane had taken his place beside her, she half turned to face him and began at the beginning.

"I knew Brian for months before we were married. I knew that he was . . . obsessed with racing. He didn't have to race to make a living, but he loved the excitement and the danger. He told me it was in his blood, and I believe it was."

She smiled suddenly. "Remember the 'groupies' on Key Largo?"

Shane nodded, eyes intent.

"Brian would have eaten that up. He was never happier than when he was surrounded by adoring racing fans."

"But you didn't like it?"

"I wasn't jealous, if that's what you mean. Jealousy over Brian was about as useful as wings on a pig. He just got a kick out of it." Her brief spurt of humor faded, and she frowned slightly. "I told you that there were problems in my marriage; that was one of them. For me to try and tie Brian down was like roping the wind—useless."

"I'm not like that, love," Shane said quietly, reaching out to take one of her hands and hold it firmly.

"You don't have to tell me that." She smiled at him mistily. Then the smile died, and her fingers closed convulsively over his.

"What is it? Tell me what you're afraid of," he begged softly.

Robyn swallowed hard and answered in a low monotone. "I'm afraid of racing, Shane. When I married Brian I was afraid. I thought that I'd learn to deal with it. But the fear grew into terror."

"Did he know?"

"He knew, but he didn't understand. He thought I was exaggerating, that I just wanted him away from the track. So I learned to keep it inside—and died a little every time he raced."

She took a deep breath and went on before Shane

could interrupt. "I thought that not knowing what was going on would help, so I stayed away from the track. Hotel rooms in different cities. I didn't watch television; I didn't listen to the radio; I just had nightmares. Wide-awake nightmares. So I tried—once—being at the track during a race. But that was worse. I felt sick, shaken. I just couldn't understand what drove Brian to risk death every time he got behind the wheel of that car.

"And it got worse. It reached a point where I couldn't even function when he raced. I just stared at the walls and waited for the phone to ring. And then—that day—something drove me to turn on the television. I saw him crash."

"Robyn—"

"I couldn't look away. The car was rolling over and over, and there was fire . . . and I knew he was dead. And do you know what the worst part was?" She stared up at Shane with blind eyes. "The worst part was that I was . . . almost . . . relieved. It was finished. What I'd been dreading had finally happened, and it was over. I didn't have to be afraid anymore—"

"Robyn!" Shane gripped her shoulders tightly. "Honey, please, stop torturing yourself!"

She blinked at him, and suddenly her eyes were clear again. "Yesterday morning . . . when we watched the sunrise?" Her voice was calm. "I'd had a nightmare. That's why I was up on deck. I dreamed that it was happening again. I was watching it happen. But this time it was you. They pulled you out of that twisted death trap. You were dead."

Robyn drew a long, shuddering breath. "Oh, God, it hurt. It's not possible to hurt that much and go on living . . ."

"Robyn." Shane's hands lifted to frame her face

gently. Unsteadily, he told her, "Honey, I wouldn't hurt you or frighten you for anything in the world. I'll stop racing. I don't need it!"

When he drew her fiercely into his arms, Robyn didn't resist. She clung to him for a long while, listening to his heart hammering beneath her cheek and realizing that he had been as disturbed by the past few minutes as she had.

Oddly, she could feel the remembered pain ebbing away. It might have been because Shane had said he wouldn't race anymore. But she didn't think so. He would race again—at least once more. He would race in the Firecracker 400 at Daytona Beach on July fourth, exactly one week from today:

"Give up something you enjoy just because I'm afraid?" Astonished at how calm her voice was, Robyn gently eased from his loosened embrace and rose to her feet, pacing over to the window before turning to face him. "I can't let you do that."

He got to his feet slowly, staring at her with frowning eyes. "You're more important to me than anything. Racing is just a hobby. I won't miss it."

She folded her arms beneath her breasts and returned his steady look. "And what else will I find to be afraid of?"

"Honey, it's a reasonable fear," he said quietly.

"If it were just fear, yes, it would be. But it's terror, Shane. Crippling terror. And if I don't face it now, learn to deal with it, then it'll only get worse."

Shane ran a distracted hand through his hair and sighed roughly. "Robyn, what are you saying?"

"That I...have to watch you race. I have to prove to myself that I can handle the fear."

"And if you can't?"

Through gritted teeth, she responded, "I will! I won't let myself be a coward. I won't smother you because I'm terrified something will happen to you!"

He was watching her very intently, a thoughtful expression on his lean face. "This is very important to you, isn't it?"

"Shane..." She took a deep breath. "I don't want to tell you to race. I want to live with you in your mountain aerie and make wine and babies. I want to grow old with you. But I have to prove to myself that I'm not a coward."

"You're not a coward, love. You hung on to your sanity for a year while your husband raced. That took courage."

"I didn't love him the way I love you. And I just don't know if I can watch you race, Shane. But I have to try. Do you understand?"

He smiled crookedly. "I think so. But, Robyn, I'm going to marry you no matter what happens. Do *you* understand?"

Robyn hesitated before replying. "One thing at a time, okay?"

His emerald eyes darkened almost to jet. "Robyn, if you're saying you won't marry me if you can't face my racing—to hell with that! I'll hang up my driving gloves, and we'll stop off in Vegas on our way to California!"

She startled herself by laughing. "Commanding sort of man, aren't you?"

"Robyn—"

She lifted a hand to cut him off. "I'm just saying that I want to think of one thing at a time."

"You're going to marry me."

Grateful for the lightened atmosphere, Robyn gave him a mock frown. "Not if you keep ordering me around like that."

"We'll make wine and babies."

"There's a population explosion."

"And you can knit little things."

"I can't knit."

"Then you can *buy* little things. Or you can *sell* little things—like books."

Robyn giggled again and immediately went to him when he smilingly held out his arms. The sense of desperation she had felt for so long was gone now, replaced by the calm determination she had felt earlier. Shane had been right; they would work it out.

He tilted her face up and kissed her. "I have to go take care of some business," he murmured huskily. "Are you going to let me stay here tonight?"

"*Let* you?" Robyn's senses whirled dizzily as she gazed into the slumbering passion and love in his eyes. "I may not let you leave in the first place!"

He chuckled softly, his eyes devouring her. "You've gotten tangled up in your own spell, haven't you, witch?"

"Looks that way." She stood on tiptoe to kiss him lightly, but ended up staying on her toes for some minutes because Shane wanted more than a light kiss. When he finally put her away from him, it was with obvious reluctance.

"If I don't leave right now, I never will," he muttered hoarsely. "And if I don't take care of Mother's business, she'll shoot me."

"You haven't done that *yet?* You mentioned being in Miami because of business a week ago!"

"I've been a bit . . . distracted."

"Your mother won't believe that."

"She will when she sees you."

Robyn smiled and reached out to trace his bottom lip with one finger. "When are you going to Daytona?"

"*We* are going tomorrow. That is, if you can get

Janie to run the store for you for another week." When she hesitated, he added quietly. "I need to have you with me, Robyn."

Immediately, she nodded. "I'll call Janie and see what we can work out. You—you will come back here after you've finished with your business?"

"Never doubt it, love." He gave her one last, possessive kiss and quickly strode toward the door. "I'll be back in a couple of hours."

Robyn stood where he'd left her, smiling, until she heard the roar of the Porsche pulling out of the drive. Then she turned slowly, staring appraisingly around the room. Mentally rolling up her sleeves, she briskly got to work.

When George dashed through the open door a few moments later, she was opening the drapes and letting sunlight into the room for the first time in months. Marty came into the room just as Robyn was throwing a pillow at the cat for sharpening his claws on the couch.

"He got into the kitchen cabinets a few minutes ago," the older woman said disapprovingly. "Spilled a box of cereal all over the floor."

"He's been a vagabond, Marty; we'll have to teach him some manners," Robyn responded vaguely, retrieving the pillow from the floor and busily plumping it up. "Do we have any packing boxes?"

"In the storage room. Why?"

Robyn waved a hand at the trophies, plaques, and photographs. "I think it's time this stuff was packed away. Don't you?"

Marty had been watching her rather intently since entering the room, but now she smiled. Apparently going off on a tangent, she murmured, "Does Mr. Shane like baked chicken? I'm fixing it for dinner tonight."

Robyn immediately caught the change in Marty's tone, including the half mocking, semi-formal address, and she knew that the relationship met with Marty's fullest approval. Smiling at the older woman, Robyn laughed. "You know, I haven't the faintest idea whether he likes baked chicken or not!"

CHAPTER
Nine

BY TWO O'CLOCK Tuesday afternoon, Robyn was busy again—unpacking in a lovely hotel suite less than half a mile from the track in Daytona Beach.

"Why did you tell me to pack lots of jeans?" she asked Shane as he hung up the phone and turned toward her. He'd been talking to Eric, and she hadn't paid any attention to the conversation.

"Because the track's not the cleanest place, and that's where we'll be all week."

Robyn felt a quick stab of panic, but curiosity overrode her instinctive reaction. "Why do I get the feeling that I'm going to learn more about racing than I ever wanted to know?" she asked warily.

Shane leaned over to fish a pair of jeans out of his own suitcase, and he waved them about instructively. "The best cure for a fear is familiarity with the object of that fear," he intoned solemnly.

"Uh huh. How sure are you of that?"

He sobered abruptly, smiling at her reassuringly. "Pretty sure. One of my sisters, Beth, was terrified of horses when she was small. Since the rest of us rode, and we didn't want her to miss out on the experience, we all worked to cure her of it. She didn't know much about horses, so we taught her. From the basics. Care and feeding, the different breeds, equipment, and so on. By the time she finally climbed into the saddle, most of her fear was gone."

"I do ride, by the way," Robyn said, mentally going over his strategy and finding it sound.

"Good. I know some terrific trails. Why are you standing there with that shirt in your hands? Move, woman! We have things to do!"

Robyn gave him a long-suffering look and continued with her unpacking. "We're not on the boat anymore; you can stop ordering me around now."

"I like ordering you around."

"I've noticed."

"If you really don't like it, you can try out one of those karate kicks like you did in the shower this morning."

"That was not a karate kick! I slipped on the damn soap, and you know it."

"Good thing I was there to catch you," he murmured.

Robyn threw a pair of her shorts at him and then dashed into the bathroom with her makeup bag before he could retaliate. Emerging to find him hanging up several of his shirts in the closet, she said, "I wonder if Marty ever found Kris. I wanted to let her know we hadn't drowned, but she wasn't home when I called."

Shane turned from the closet with laughter gleaming in his eyes. "I think you'd better sit down," he warned gravely.

Automatically, she sank down onto the foot of the bed. "Why? Is something going on?"

He appeared to consider the thought. "I would say so. Definitely."

"Well, what?"

"It's about Kris. And why she wasn't there to answer the phone."

Robyn eyed him suspiciously. "You appear to be hugely enjoying yourself. Why wasn't Kris there to answer the phone?"

"Because she's here."

"In Daytona?" she asked blankly. "Why would she be here?"

Shane smiled gently. "Remember Eric?" he quizzed.

Robyn stared at him for a long moment with slowly widening eyes. "Eric? She's here with Eric?"

"Well, you told me to give him her number. Apparently, they really hit it off."

"If she's here with him, I guess they did." Robyn shook her head dazedly. "Is it serious, do you think?"

"Judging by Eric's voice, it is. I've never heard him sound so happy. There may well be two weddings in the offing."

"They haven't known each other a week!"

"Does that matter?" Shane asked softly.

Looking at the man she had known less than two weeks, Robyn smiled slowly. "No. That doesn't matter at all."

Slightly more than an hour later, Robyn was trying to get straight in her mind the names of the men in Shane's pit crew. There were half a dozen of them, and the only one she could remember was Shorty—

who was nearly a head taller than Shane and thin as a rail.

They were all at the track, and Shane was "starting with the basics." After introducing her to the men, he calmly put her behind the wheel of his car, a gleaming Thunderbird, and began explaining all the safety features.

At first nervous, Robyn quickly became interested enough to pay close attention. She was surprised to find that the car was actually much safer than the one she drove to work each morning; but she reminded herself that it was a machine pushed to the highest speeds and structurally strained to the limits on the racetrack.

Still, it was reassuring to find that Shane took safety very seriously. He explained the checklist he went over before each race and briefly touched on the amount of work constantly done on the car to keep it in top shape.

The work was going on as they sat there, and Robyn got out of the car—with a little help from Shane, since the door wouldn't open—and walked around to the open hood to see what was going on. She peered into the car's innards, frowning slightly.

"Routine maintenance." Shane had come up behind her. "Right now, he's—"

"I know," she said. "He's adjusting the carburetor."

Shane turned her around to face him. "You are the most amazing mixture of ignorance and gold! You've been holding out on me again, haven't you?" he accused softly.

"Not really." She smiled up at him. "I'm an Army brat, remember? And my father's only offspring. Naturally, I was given the benefit of his teachings. So I do know one end of a car from the other. As a matter of fact, I can tinker with the best of them."

"Change a tire?"

"Or the oil. I even overhauled a transmission once."

"Then why am I paying these lazy bums?" Shane sent a mocking glare toward Shorty, still bent under the hood of the T-Bird. "I'll just hire you."

Robyn shook her head as Shorty chuckled softly. "No way. I don't know anything about race cars. Besides, I'd ruin my nails."

"Women!" Shane rolled his eyes heavenward.

"Uh uh. Woman. Singular."

"I'll go along with that."

Robyn didn't feel the slightest bit of embarrassment as Shane kissed her in front of half a dozen grinning, coveralled men. In fact, she returned the embrace with great enthusiasm.

"Hello? Will you look at that? It's indecent!"

With her arms still around Shane's waist, Robyn leaned sideways to peer past him at Kris and Eric, who had just arrived. "Hello. When did you blow into town?" she asked pleasantly.

"Over the weekend," Kris informed her with equal aplomb.

Looking at her cousin's glowing face and Eric's happy smile—and their entwined hands—Robyn lifted an eyebrow. "That was fast work," she commented teasingly. "I've never seen such fatuous expressions in my life!"

"Try looking in a mirror!" Kris retorted.

Robyn kept one arm around Shane's slim waist as he turned to greet the new arrivals. When Eric immediately began talking about some problem with one of Shane's sponsors, Kris took her cousin's hand and drew her a little apart from the hubbub surrounding the car.

"Robyn, you're going to let him race?"

"What choice do I have?" Robyn was watching Shane.

"Are you kidding? Shane adores you; anybody could see that. He'd do anything for you!"

Robyn transferred her gaze to Kris's worried face. "And I'd do anything for him." Her voice was smooth. "I have to let him race, Kris. I have to know that I can take it, that I won't smother him with my own stupid fears."

Kris stared at her for a long silent moment. "And how will Shane feel," she pressed quietly, "when he has to watch you suffer? He won't do it, Robyn. I think he'll quit whether you can take it or not."

Running damp palms down the thighs of her faded jeans, Robyn met Kris's look, telling herself that her cousin was right about one thing: Shane wouldn't let her suffer if he could help it. His love for her made him as protective as her love for him made her. And she thought with remorse of the fear she had put him through because she'd been reluctant to explain her own fears.

"He won't watch me suffer," she told Kris flatly, fierce determination straightening her shoulders. "Because I *won't* suffer. I won't do that to myself anymore. I won't do that to us."

"You *could* take the easy route, you know," Kris pointed out.

Robyn sighed. "I've taken the line of least resistance all my life. I think it's time I grew up."

"Secrets, ladies?" Shane draped an arm around Robyn's shoulders and smiled down at her.

"We're plotting your downfall, of course," Kris supplied instantly.

"It's a little late for that." Shane grinned as he watched his friend take the hand of his own lady, and then he shook his head in mock sorrow. "You two ladies plotted far too well in the beginning. We've fallen about as far as we can fall."

"She plotted." Robyn sent a demure glance up at Shane. "I cast spells."

"You don't have to remind me of that, witch!" Shane chuckled softly. "I'll never be the same again."

"And aren't you glad—"

"Glad? What man happily welcomes insanity?" Shane retorted.

Eric interrupted as Robyn was playfully trying to strangle her favorite dragonslayer. "As much as I hate to put an end to this little scene," he said dryly, "I'm afraid I have to. Shane, Jordan's threatening dire things if you don't present yourself this afternoon. And since he *is* your biggest sponsor . . ."

"What's he afraid I'll do—run off with the car?"

"Ask him. I'm just passing the message along."

Shane sighed. "All right, then." He winked at Robyn. "Come along with me, witch. I'll introduce you."

"Like this?" She looked down at her jeans and casual top. "I'm not dressed to meet sponsors!"

"Nonsense. You'll melt his crusty, money-grubbing little heart."

"Oh no. You can't hide behind me. I'm not big enough!"

"You'll be all he'll see . . ." Shane purred.

As the week wore on, Robyn found that she was actually enjoying spending most of her time in the large open garage, smelling grease and oil and fuel, listening to men calling out to one another, and growing accustomed to the clank of tools and the roar of engines.

It had never occurred to Brian to ease her fear by exposing her to racing, by giving her a behind-the-scenes look at the sport. And Robyn had wanted no part of it then. But she was determined to learn now, and learn she did.

She sat in on strategy meetings with Shane, Eric, and the "foreman" of the pit crew, Sonny, who was middle-aged, stout, and had a weatherbeaten face and shrewd gray eyes. Silently, she listened as they discussed which drivers would likely be racing and what their habits were.

Shane put her behind the wheel of the T-Bird one day and had her drive once around the track by herself. Vaguely worried that he was breaking a rule by having her do that, Robyn nonetheless found herself fascinated by this new perspective. The audible power of the car made her a bit uneasy, but when it responded instantly to even her inexperienced hand, she relaxed and enjoyed the brief trip.

She met the representatives of various sponsors, learned the names of everyone in the pit crew, and was introduced to sports reporters as Shane's "lady."

Inevitably, "lady" stuck. Whenever Shane came back into the garage after being absent for some reason, his first words would be: "Where's my lady?" If Robyn wasn't immediately produced, he'd keep asking until somebody found her. After the track was nearly turned upside down one day—Robyn and Kris had gone for hamburgers and forgotten to tell anyone—Sonny made it his business always to know where Shane's lady was so he wouldn't be yelled at.

And the entire crew called her Lady as if it were her name.

"You'll always be Lady to them," Kris remarked once in amusement.

"I know. Isn't it sweet?"

Robyn was a bit puzzled, though, at the careful, respectful way the men treated her. Having been an

Army brat, she knew very well that when groups of men worked together, there was always a great deal of good-natured roughness, swearing, and rather ribald teasing. That wouldn't have bothered her in the least.

Being wrapped in cotton wool did.

While Shane was in a meeting with track officials on Thursday morning, Robyn cornered Eric to demand what was going on. She found him seated behind a table that served as a makeshift desk, paying far more attention to the blonde in his lap than to the papers spread out before him.

"Excuse me?" Robyn said politely.

Eric, like Shane, was not easily embarrassed. He simply lifted his head, leisurely, and stared at Robyn. "Yes?" he queried with equally bland politeness.

"What's going on?" Robyn leaned her palms on the table and tactfully ignored the flush on her cousin's face. "Shorty nearly had a heart attack when he almost ran into me a minute ago. And Sonny hovers over me like a mother hen. Why am I being treated like I'm made of porcelain?"

Kris giggled, and Eric's lips twitched. "That's Shane's fault, I'm afraid," he confessed.

"What did Shane do?" Robyn asked blankly.

"Put the fear of God into them!" Kris laughed.

"I beg your pardon?" Robyn looked from one to the other.

"Shane had a talk with the men," Eric drawled, amusement in his light blue eyes. "The gist of which was that if any one of them hurt, frightened, embarrassed, or otherwise disturbed you, he would be quite displeased. So displeased that he would very likely tie the offender to the rear bumper of his car and drive around the track a few thousand times."

Robyn found that her mouth was hanging open,

and she hastily closed it. "Well, no wonder I'm being treated like a leper," she muttered. "Don't tell me they believed him?"

"I would have if I'd been in their shoes," Eric replied.

Torn between being warmed by Shane's concern and amused at the situation he had created, Robyn shook her head slowly. "It's got to stop. I'm going to be underfoot for a while at least, and they won't be able to get any work done if they're terrified of tripping over me."

"Sit in a corner." Kris suggested with a grin.

"Then I *would* be treated like porcelain." Robyn frowned thoughtfully. "No, I'll try something else." Without another word to the amused couple watching her, she turned and made her way back to the car.

She watched the activity for a while, then looked down at her shorts and sweatshirt with a faint grimace. Well, she wasn't exactly dressed for it, but she wasn't about to go on being treated like a delicate doll if she could help it. Pushing up the sleeves of her shirt, she set about making herself useful.

For the first hour or so, the men greeted her attempts with bemused wariness, but things rapidly loosened up when they discovered that she knew what she was doing. Amusement grew when she dropped a wrench and swore violently, and when she teased Shorty because he turned red every time she spoke to him.

By the time she had recalled several slightly off-color jokes from her Army days and busily replaced three spark plugs, she was well on her way to being everyone's kid sister.

"Hand me that wrench, Lady, will you?"

"Not that way, Lady—turn it to the left. Yeah, like that."

"I'll toss you to see who goes for lunch. What do you mean, you'll flip the coin? I don't trust you. Shane probably gave you his two-headed quarter!"

"Your father was in the Army? I remember once . . ."

"No, Lady, Shane won't be mad because you sat on his hat. It was his fault for leaving it on the seat anyway."

"And then the General's wife . . ."

"Lady, toss me that filter, will you? I said *toss* it— don't sail it like a Frisbee!"

"No, Shorty doesn't mind getting oil in his eye. Tell Lady you don't mind getting oil in your eye, Shorty. Shorty? Of course he didn't drown. People don't drown in oil. Shorty?"

"And she shoved him out the window because the General was coming, but the bedroom was on the second floor, so . . ."

"Lady, put your hair up under this cap. No, the sponsor won't mind. Besides, it never looked that good on Shane."

"The drive shaft's connected to the . . . Hey, Sonny, what's the drive shaft connected to?"

"Hell, you mean you don't know? Uh oh, we're all in trouble."

". . . and he wanted to know how Joe had managed to break his leg on level ground right beneath the General's window . . ."

"Here, Lady, you can't lift that. Let me. Wait a minute—I can't lift it, either. Shorty? Shorty! Of course he's not hiding from you, Lady."

". . . and the General never could understand why that pair of shoes under the bed didn't fit him."

"Paul, hand Lady that hose . . . Because her hands are smaller and she can get it into place better than I can."

"No, Shorty didn't mind that you stepped on his

toes. He shouldn't have been standing there. You didn't mind, did you, Shorty?"

"Lady, take this rag and put it in your pocket; you shouldn't wipe your hands on your shirt. No pockets? Then...yeah, do that. You look like an Arab with it draped over your cap."

"...so this Captain walked in one day, and..."

"Here, I'll give you a boost. Crank her up and let's hear how she sounds."

"Of course there's no radio. This is a *race* car."

"...the base PX just didn't have what he wanted, so..."

"Lady, Shorty's eye isn't black. That's the oil from before. And he knows you didn't *mean* to hit him with your elbow. It was all his fault. It was all your fault, wasn't it, Shorty?"

"...so the Captain says..."

Kris wandered in sometime during the morning and watched with wide eyes, shaking her head when Robyn winked at her. She headed back toward Eric, apparently to report the changed attitude among the crew.

When Shane finally got back, Robyn was flat on her back on a wooden creeper underneath the car, helping Shorty.

"Where's my lady?"

She heard Shane's bellow and the answering rumble of male voices. She peered sideways and saw his feet stop beside her own.

"What *are* you doing under there?"

"How do you know it's me?" she asked loftily. "I could be somebody else."

Shane's foot nudged her bare ankle. "Nobody else has legs like these. Why are you trysting with Shorty under the car?"

"I'm not trysting. I'm ruining my nails."

Shane bent down to grasp her ankle, pulling her and the creeper out from under the car. He took the wrench out of her hand, pulled her to her feet, and sent the creeper rolling away with a thrust of his foot. Then he stared at her.

"Should I ask why you're wearing a cloth over your hat? Or why you're wearing *my* hat? Or why you have a smudge of grease on your nose?" His voice was solemn.

"No."

He sighed and pulled the cloth off her hat. Using the cloth to wipe the grease away, he said, "I seem to spend half my time either putting something on your nose or taking something off it. Why didn't you put on a pair of coveralls if you wanted to tinker?"

"Sonny found three pairs, and I got lost in all of them. Apparently, there aren't many small mechanics."

"Fancy that." He tossed the cloth aside and then pulled off the hat and tossed it aside, too. Abruptly serious, his emerald eyes searched hers intently. "Are you all right, honey? Really all right?"

Robyn smiled and stood on tiptoe to link her arms around his neck. "I'm really all right," she confirmed softly. She smiled sunnily. "But I think Shorty wants to talk to you about a raise..."

As the qualifying laps scheduled for Saturday and Sunday drew near, tension increased noticeably among the men. Activity picked up around the track as all the cars arrived, and the place was hectic with noise and semi-organized confusion. Reporters multiplied in number, and flashbulbs began going off unexpectedly.

Robyn felt the growing tension but refused to let

it get to her. The days and nights spent with Shane had given her something very precious to hold on to, and her determination to conquer her fear remained fixed in her mind.

She knew that Shane was watching her carefully, knew that he would instantly withdraw from the race if she showed any signs of the torturing fear. That she showed no signs had nothing to do with her ability to pretend; it was impossible to hide her feelings from him.

But somehow, she had gained strength from Shane and from their love. Knowing that he supported her fully, she was able to look at her fear, for the first time, rationally.

Why had she been so terrified of Brian's racing? Because she had loved him, certainly. But there had been more to it than that. From the very beginning, racing had possessed more of Brian than she had. It had been worse than his infidelity would have been. She could have fought another woman; she couldn't fight a car.

Because racing had possessed so much of Brian, she had convinced herself that it would take all of him. As she had gone with him from city to city, race to race, he had become more and more possessed with the determination to win every time. He had hungered for the Winston Cup, NASCAR's top award, the way another man might have hungered for the woman of his dreams.

And Robyn had grown more terrified.

A normal, reasonable fear of high speeds and danger, coupled with the memory of her father's death at the hands of a drunk driver, had grown into something all-consuming.

Safe in the haven of Shane's love, Robyn looked back on her fear with detached analytical interest.

What had frightened her the most? That Brian would be killed? Or that she was becoming a vague shadow by his side, unimportant, unneeded? Lost in the wake of a speeding car.

Quiet fear, loneliness, resentment, jealousy, ignorance of the sport, hatred of it—all had twisted into terror. A terror she had been unable to fight, even to understand, because there had been no solid foundation to stand on. There had been no loving arms to hold her close at night, at morning, at mid-afternoon. No booming voice demanding to know where his lady was.

How much laughter had she shared with Brian? How many times had she awakened, cold and lonely, with nothing to hold but her growing fear? How many times had a quiet instinct deep inside her murmured that Brian would have been just as happy with another woman, just as pleased by another body in his bed?

He had never worried over her fears. He had never introduced her to sponsors or reporters with possessive pride. He had never looked at her with eyes that said she meant everything to him, or silently shared the heart-stopping beauty of a sunrise.

Why had Brian's racing terrified her? Not because she had loved him. Because he had not loved her.

Robyn allowed the realization to sink slowly into her mind, her heart. Brian had never truly loved her. A little sadly, she understood at last that he had been unable to love her the way she had needed to be loved.

He had been her husband in name, in fact. But he had never really been her lover. And certainly never a friend. And she had never been a wife to him, because he hadn't needed a wife.

But Shane? He was her friend, her lover. He teased her and laughed with her—and held up a mirror to her soul. He was her match, her equal, on some level she couldn't name. The other half of herself, the part that made her complete.

She was necessary to Shane, just as he was to her. His delight in her, in what they had found together, told her over and over again how much she meant to him. With him she had found the companionship she had longed for, the love she had needed.

A mutual love.

For the first time in her life, Robyn completely understood herself. And she knew then that she would be able to watch Shane race, that fear wouldn't cripple her—not because she didn't love him enough, but because he loved her enough. Shane didn't need racing to make him happy, but he needed her. What had he told her only moments after setting eyes on her? That he had dreamed her. That he had always dreamed her.

In that moment, Robyn had felt that she knew him, that she had always known him. She had blamed some fleeting resemblance to Brian and convinced herself that she had wanted one last night with her husband.

But the strange shock she had felt had had nothing to do with a memory of Brian. Wistfully, she had dreamed the encounter the way it might have been between her and Brian. Might have been, but never was. The searing passion and shivering tenderness, the sensation that it was only the two of them alone in a world of magic. The knowledge that everything was forgotten in the wonder of love.

Only Shane's determined pursuit had shown her that her dream had contained not the ghost of her husband, but the living, breathing body of the stranger she had tumbled headlong into love with.

The man she had dreamed of. Always dreamed of.

Racing would never take Shane away from her. Not in this life, and not in the next. He belonged fully to her, just as she belonged completely to him. They would make wine and babies together, and grow old together. And though they would be apart for brief times in the flesh, they would never be apart in spirit.

This new understanding brought a serene glow to Robyn's eyes—at least, that's what the reporters wrote in their "human interest" stories about this woman who had lost one man to racing and was now involved with another.

The enterprising reporter who had dug into Robyn's past and unearthed her marriage to Brian McAllaster tried to interview her, but Shane's constant presence seemed to cramp his style. And since Robyn was only mildly amused by the interest in her past, she said little. So the reporter wove about Robyn's surprised person a tale of love and sacrifice and courage that made Joan of Arc pale by comparison.

Safe in her newly discovered strength, Robyn was able to laugh and shake her head over the story. She tried to explain to the reporter that he was dramatizing things a bit, but he was hot on the trail of what seemed likely to be the most talked about story at that year's Firecracker 400.

It wasn't until his next story appeared in Saturday's newspaper that Shane discovered that Robyn's father had been killed in a car wreck three years before.

"Dammit, why didn't you tell me?"

"It's been three years, darling. It doesn't hurt anymore."

Shane faced her as they stood in their hotel suite late Saturday afternoon. "You should have told me," he said roughly. "How did it happen?"

"Another driver had had too much New Year's cheer. His car crossed the median and crashed into Daddy's."

Shane looked at her searchingly. "I can pull out, honey. It's not too late."

Robyn smiled at him and calmly began unbuttoning her shirt. "Nonsense," she murmured. "You're going to qualify tomorrow, and on Monday you're going to win the race."

His eyes darkened as he watched her dispose of the shirt. "What are you doing?" he gasped.

"Sharpening my vamping abilities. I've nearly gotten them honed to a fine edge, wouldn't you say?"

"I'd say. But aren't we supposed to meet Eric and Kris in the lobby half an hour from now?"

"I think they'll be late. I think we will be, too." Robyn paused for a moment to regard him with a mock frown. "Or should we be conserving your energy? Jocks in training—"

"I'm not a jock," Shane interrupted hastily, moving toward her with desire flaring in his eyes.

"Oh, well. Then we needn't worry."

Sunday afternoon was hot and still when Robyn took her place in the stands to watch Shane drive the necessary qualifying laps around the track. She was aware of her friends' searching glances, but her entire attention was fixed on the Thunderbird rolling out onto the track. It was colorful with the decals of sponsors, and gleaming from the washing the crew had given it only an hour before.

Long moments later, she was turning away from the railing and heading for the pit area. Elation surged through her as she realized that her strongest emotions while watching Shane's car tearing around the track had been excitement and pride.

She was barely aware of Kris and Eric following behind her as she hurried to be in the pit when Shane arrived. She got there just as the car did, and she watched as Shane was helped from the vehicle. He tossed his protective helmet to one of the crew, and emerald eyes immediately searched the small crowd.

"Where's my lady?"

Robyn launched herself from three feet away and was instantly caught in strong arms and swung in a happy circle. "There's my lady," he murmured, utter satisfaction in his voice as he gazed down at her. He kissed her possessively, apparently oblivious to their interested spectators.

"That's showing 'em how, skipper," Robyn said when she finally found the breath for it.

"On the track?" He lifted an inquiring eyebrow. "Or here?"

"Oh, both." Ignoring the chuckles around them, she added softly, "They should see what you can do on the sea..."

CHAPTER
Ten

THE QUALIFYING LAPS hadn't frightened Robyn. The race did. She had expected the fear, and she was ready for it. It was sane, rational fear. Shane was driving a car surrounded by other cars in a close pack at speeds in excess of a hundred and fifty miles per hour.

The slightest mistake in judgement on his part, or on the part of even one other driver, could end in tragedy. The grueling pace demanded endurance from both man and machine.

As Monday afternoon wore on, several cars dropped out of the race because of mechanical failure. Heat shimmered above the track, and the roar of laboring engines drowned out every other sound.

Rather than watching the race from the stands, Robyn remained in the pit area. She was there to smile at Shane and give him a brief thumbs-up signal each time he pulled the T-Bird in for a bewilderingly quick change of tires and refueling.

A quick smile and flash of emerald eyes, and he was back on the track again.

There was only one mishap during the afternoon, and it wasn't serious, although it easily could have been. A car blew its engine coming off a turn, and the cars behind it narrowly avoided a collision. One of those cars was Shane's Thunderbird.

Robyn's heart leaped into her throat and hung for an agonizing second until the hazard was safely passed.

"Are you all right?"

She turned her head to find both Eric and Kris watching her carefully, and she knew without being told that Shane had asked them to keep an eye on her.

"I'm fine," she said faintly.

"It isn't easy, is it?" Kris empathized.

"No." Robyn turned her eyes back to the track and rapidly found Shane's car among the others. "No, it isn't easy."

Her heart jumped into her throat more than once during that long afternoon. The courage she had gained during the past few days held—just. Her eyes remained fixed on the T-Bird with almost hypnotic intensity. But an unfamiliar excitement gripped her as Shane established a lead late in the afternoon and doggedly held it.

By the closing moments of the race, the lead had narrowed to one lap, and two more cars blew their engines in a last vain effort to close the gap. When the checkered flag waved above the finish line, it was to signal Shane's victory.

Robyn didn't need Eric's guiding arm to take her to Shane. By instinct, she was heading to meet the Thunderbird as it rolled in. The car was surrounded by jubilant fans and well-wishers, all trying to touch

Shane and congratulate him. The loudspeaker was blaring, and the crowd was roaring.

The pit crew managed to cut their way through the confusion of people and help Shane from the car. Flashbulbs were popping all around them, and the din of excited voices filled the air. But his deep voice rose easily above all the chatter.

"Where's my lady?"

He had tossed his helmet aside, and the grime of the long hot hours in the car streaked his weary face. But the emerald eyes were bright with a touching eagerness as they scanned the crowd.

And his lady flung herself into his arms.

It was hours later before Eric and Kris had shoved the last well-wisher out the door and bid Robyn and Shane good night. Looking around their suite at the clutter left behind from the impromptu party, Robyn shook her head in amusement.

"We'd better call the maid."

"In the morning." Smiling down at her, Shane reached out to draw her into his arms. "I haven't had a moment alone with you all day."

"You've been busy," Robyn excused. She laced her fingers together at the back of his neck, happily breathing in the clean, spicy scent of his aftershave. "You barely had time to shower and accept the sponsors' congratulations before the fans started arriving."

"Mmmm." Shane lifted an inquiring brow. "I noticed that wacky blonde showed up. What did you say to her that took the wind out of her sails so quickly?"

"Nothing much." Robyn smiled up at him, remembering the girl from Key Largo and their little confrontation today. "Just that I was going to make an honest man out of you."

His arms tightened around her. "And are you?" he

asked huskily, emerald eyes flaring with unconcealed hope.

"Was there any doubt?" Robyn felt her heart lurch with sudden, overpowering love as she met the searching look. "I'm an old-fashioned kind of girl, skipper; you'll just have to marry me."

"Nobody has to point a shotgun at me, honey," he told her gruffly, giving her a bone-crushing hug. "I've wanted to marry you since the moment I set eyes on you!"

"And here I had to do the asking!"

"I asked you more than a week ago!"

Suddenly serious, Robyn looked up at him gravely. "I had to find out a few things about myself before I could answer you," she explained quietly.

"If you could handle the racing?"

"That, and why I was so afraid in the first place. I didn't understand that fear, Shane, and I needed to."

"And you understand now?" he asked, a hint of anxiety in his vivid eyes.

She nodded, smiling as she gazed up at him. "I understand now. I thought that I was terrified of racing, Shane, but that was never the real fear; the real fear was a fear of loss."

Shane pulled her a bit closer, as if to combat that fear. "Loss? You mean because racing is dangerous?"

"Not exactly. It all started with Brian." Her eyes asked his understanding of this last mention of her husband, and Shane nodded silently as he read the question there.

Robyn sighed softly. "I told you once that Brian was obsessed with racing. And I mean just that. He had to win every race; it took up his whole life. Racing had more of him than I could ever have had, and that scared me to death. I think that what frightened me the most wasn't that Brian could have been killed. What unnerved me was that I was becoming nothing more than a shadow in his life. My relationship with Brian was so empty, all I had to hold on to was the fear. Does that make sense?"

Shane smiled gently down at her. "It makes sense."

Robyn returned the smile, gazing up at her friend, her lover. "Once I understood that racing wouldn't take you away from me, I knew I could watch you race," she whispered. Her smile turned rueful. "I won't like it, but I can take it."

"You won't have to."

She stared at him uncertainly, feeling a sudden surge of hope. "Shane, don't give up racing for me. Please."

"I'm not, honey." His smile was a little crooked. "I'm giving it up for me."

"But you love it!"

"I love you more." He shook his head. "Robyn, I never needed racing. It was just a hobby, something to occupy my time and energy. I liked winning, I'll admit. But I always intended to go back to being a full-time vintner; I never wanted to be written up in the record books as the best driver of all time.

"And when I was out there today, seeing you waiting for me every time I pulled into the pits, I realized that I'd never race again. I'd be a fool to risk everything I have by climbing into that car again. And I wouldn't lose you for all the fame and money in the world. Today was my swan song."

Robyn was afraid to hope, afraid to show him how much she hoped. She didn't want him to race. She didn't want him to spend precious hours risking his life. But she loved him enough to watch him, if that was what he wanted.

But now he was saying...

Shane framed her face with his warm hands. "Oh, witch-lady," he murmured, "don't you know even yet how much I love you? I lost my soul in your eyes the first night we met. The night I couldn't believe my luck, because I was dancing with the woman who had haunted my dreams for years—for always.

"And she looked up at me as though the spell had caught her, too; as if she knew, without words or stupid games, that we belonged together. She left that boring party with me, putting her hand in mine with such complete trust that it made my heart ache."

He laughed softly as he gazed with darkened eyes at her dazed expression. "My feet never touched the ground that night. I had found a treasure, and I would have fought demons from hell to keep her. She showed me an enchanted place I had never believed possible, a land of lovers and dreamers."

Bending his head, he rubbed his forehead against hers gently. "And then she was gone the next morning." His breath was soft as a whisper on her face. "Like a dream. And I think I went a little crazy. I had to find her...because she was the other half of myself, the part that made me real."

Robyn swallowed hard, and managed to whisper, "And then you heard I was married."

Shane nodded slowly, the green eyes darkening and darkening until they were very nearly black. "I wanted to take you away from your husband," he confessed thickly, a muscle tightening suddenly in his jaw. "And at the same time, I felt betrayed, wounded, because I thought you belonged to him.

"When you told me you were a widow, the relief was staggering. I almost told you then that I loved you, but I could see that you were wary of me. I had to find out why. I thought that you were still in love with your husband, and that made it all the more bewildering."

Robyn was suddenly, crushingly aware of how much she must have hurt him. "And when I lied to you— Oh, darling, I'm so sorry!"

"I frightened you." His voice was low, far away, as though he were reliving that terrible moment, and his eyes were as opaque as those of a blind man. "I never wanted to frighten you, honey. But I wasn't...quite sane. The thought that you had pretended I was your husband..."

"I love you, Shane," she whispered fiercely, putting her heart and soul into the words, trying to make up for the other words that should never have been uttered. Trying to erase a lie told to herself and to him.

"I knew that night that I had sent you away hating me because I was too scared to think about a future with you racing. I was so afraid of loving you. And it all happened so quickly! It almost didn't seem real." She looked up at him with pain and regret in her eyes. "How could you go on loving me after that night?"

"What choice did I have?" he asked simply, a faint smile lifting the corners of his mouth. "I could no more stop loving you than I could stop breathing."

"Oh, Shane." She stood on tiptoe to reach his mouth, wanting to reassure him, wanting to belong to him now, with everything cleared up between them.

His kiss was filled with half savage tenderness, with love and possession and need. He kissed her as though the world would end at any moment and he wanted the touch and taste of her to be the memory he carried with him into eternity.

Robyn lost herself in a surge of sensations and emotions. She felt a wild, primitive craving to merge with him and become one being. His kiss seemed to draw her very soul from her body to join his in some heaven only they knew.

She felt him lift her into his arms and carry her toward the bedroom with easy strength. Her arms locked around his neck, Robyn clung to him, dazed, needing him as she had never needed him before. She was in a dream once again—the dream, the reality, of Shane's love.

He set her gently on her feet by the huge, lamplit bed, gazing down on her with emerald fires burning in his eyes. "No more questions?" he whispered. "No more fears?"

"No questions, no fears," she answered huskily. "I love you, Shane. With everything inside me."

Shane bent his head to kiss her gently, his lips moving from her mouth to caress her throat and the hollows beneath her ears. Nimble fingers slowly began to unfasten her blouse, one button at a time, with infinite care. His hands softly touched bared golden flesh as a caressing tongue circled the tiny heartbeat pounding away at the base of her neck.

And Robyn's hands were far from still. She eagerly parted the buttons on his shirt, touching his firm chest as if hungry for the sensation. She pressed her lips briefly to him, tasting his clean skin as he pushed her blouse off her shoulders. Immediately, her hands returned to tug his shirt from the waistband of his slacks and help him shrug it off.

He unclasped her bra and smoothed it away, shaping her breasts almost wonderingly, thumbs teasing the rosy peaks to vibrant awareness. "You were made for me," he told her hoarsely, his opened mouth drifting over her closed eyelids. "Beautiful witch, you fit me so well . . ."

Robyn traced the rippling muscles of his back. She

felt a tremor shake his strong frame, and an aching trembling began in the center of her being. With a catch of her breath, she reached for the waistband of his slacks, desperate to touch him totally.

She unfastened the snap and tugged the zipper down, her mouth moving in a rhythmical back-and-forth motion across his broad chest as she slowly slid the pants down over lean hips, strong thighs.

He kicked the jumble of clothing away, reaching for the snap of her jeans and groaning softly as her fingers teased and caressed with the certain knowledge of him that the last week had given her.

Her jeans fell away from her and she was lifted and placed tenderly on the bed. Strong hands brushed away the final barrier of her thin nylon panties, and then he was lying beside her on the wide bed.

"God, I need you," he rasped softly. "I'll always need you." He touched her face as though reading Braille, tracing the curve of her brows, her nose, her slightly parted lips. Sensitive fingers moved in a butterfly caress over her skin.

Robyn caught his finger as it passed gently over her lips, letting him feel the sharp edge of her teeth, staring up at him with eyes full of need. Her hands came up to clasp his wrists, feeling a pulse hammering beneath the skin. "Shane," she breathed, more emotion than she would have believed possible contained in the single word.

He lifted her hands to his mouth, pressing soft, tender kisses along each finger, touching his tongue lightly to her palms. He gazed down at her, his hunger written vividly on his face. "I love you, witch," he murmured deeply before his mouth lowered, hotly capturing a throbbing nipple.

She moaned softly, feeling the wet warmth of his

lips, the tongue swirling avidly. She tangled her fingers in his dark hair, her legs moving restlessly until they were trapped by one of his. Rough hands explored her body in long strokes and then settled to tease, to incite.

Robyn explored his body fervently, breathing shallowly, feeling the splintering tension building within her. "Shane!" She heard herself pleading with him in a drugged voice. "Love me, darling, please love me!"

Shane needed no further urging. He rose above her, settling himself between her thighs like a man coming home. For a long moment, he was still, with her, holding her, kissing her with burning tenderness. Then he lifted his head to gaze into her rapt eyes as he slowly began to move.

Robyn moved with him eagerly, gasping out her love for him, the desire that never seemed to diminish transporting her higher than ever before. She held him with muscles she hadn't realized she possessed, and she saw the surprise and excitement flicker in his eyes and grip his taut features.

Their movements became faster, heated, the primitive drive for release overpowering rational thought. Instinct took over, and both gave selflessly of themselves. Muffled words of love filled the lamplit room, and then the world disappeared. They were, for the brief, timeless moment allowed to mortals, one being.

They lay together at last, limp, exhausted. But not quite sated. Never quite sated. As though they feared that they were about to be parted, they kissed tenderly, lovingly.

Robyn could feel his hands unsteadily stroking her back, her hair, as if he couldn't stop touching her. She found her own hands smoothing tanned flesh, tugging gently at the crisp dark hair covering his chest.

"I love you, skipper," she murmured in a contented voice.

"I love you, too, witch-lady," he vowed softly, his hands still shaping her slender body. "Always and forever."

She cuddled even closer, murmuring a sleepy protest when he disengaged them enough to reach down and pull the covers up over their bodies.

"Get the light, witch," he murmured, drawing her close again.

Robyn waved a vague hand in the direction of the lamp. "Light. Abracadabra."

"It didn't work," he told her. "Try another charm."

"Shall I twitch my nose?"

"Whatever."

Robyn reached up to rub her nose—mainly because the hair on his chest was tickling it. "Didn't work."

"Try something else."

"Open sesame."

"That's for doors."

"Who's the witch here?"

"I'm beginning to wonder."

"I got you, didn't I?"

"There is that."

"Then don't question my spells."

"I beg your pardon." His voice held a laugh. "But the light's still on."

"How do you expect me to cast spells when I've barely got the energy to breathe?" Robyn sighed languidly. "Which reminds me—for a man who drove an exhausting race today, your energy level is amazing. What's your secret? Vitamin E? Wheaties?"

"Neither. A demanding witch in my bed."

"I am not demanding." She couldn't even summon the energy to be decently indignant.

"Of course you are." He dropped a kiss on the top of her head. "That's all right, though. I like being demanded."

"Actually, I just have this thing for dragonslayers."

"With mountain aeries?"

"With mountain aeries. Dragonslayers who go out at night to dig up litter boxes for stray cats, and buy stuffed dolphins, and lead helpless women around by their braids. It's a quirk in my nature."

"I have a quirk, too."

"You have several."

"Funny."

Robyn squeaked as a gently punishing hand smacked her bottom. "Sorry. What's your quirk?"

"Yellow-eyed witches. Shall we fly to California on your broomstick, or will you condescend to use a plane?"

"What are we going to do with my store, my house, Marty, and King George?" she asked pointedly.

"Sell the house and the store and ship the rest to Napa Valley. Unless you'd like to keep the house."

"What woman needs a Spanish style house in Florida when she's got a mountain aerie in California? We'll sell the house. Do you really not mind Marty coming with us? She's been with me for so long now..."

"Of course not." He erased doubts with a swift hug. "The aerie has plenty of room. And people read in Napa Valley when they're not stamping grapes, so—"

"I'd like to watch you stamp grapes," she interrupted wistfully. "With your pants legs rolled up and your feet turning purple."

He chuckled softly. "We don't do it that way anymore. But if you like, we'll order a bushel of grapes in the morning, pour them into the bathtub, and stamp away."

"Will we make wine?"

"We'll make a mess; I don't know about wine."

"Never mind. I'll wait until we get to California, and you can show me how it's really done. Will George like your aerie?"

"Our aerie. There are plenty of trees to climb."

"He'll love it." Robyn sighed and absently traced a finger along his firm jaw. A sudden thought occurred to her, and she murmured uneasily, "Your family. Won't they be upset that you've suddenly decided to marry a woman they haven't even met?"

"They've had a week to get used to the idea," he told her with utter calm. "I called them from Miami."

"You what?" Robyn finally managed to lift her head, staring down at him in surprise. "When?"

"Before I came back to your place last Monday night. I called Mother, and I'm sure she's told everyone else."

"*What* did you tell her?" Robyn demanded suspiciously.

"The truth, of course." He finally opened his eyes to return her uneasy look with one brimming with laughter. "That I'd fallen under the spell of a beautiful witch, and that I planned to marry her just as soon as I could drag her to the altar."

"Oh, Lord," Robyn muttered.

"Don't look so nervous. You'll love Mother. She told me not to lose you between Florida and California, and started planning the wedding. Huge, she decided."

"Shane, I can't let her do that! It's supposed to be the bride's family that throws the wedding, and besides, you don't want all that fuss and bother—"

"Are you kidding?" He pulled her over fully on top of him. "I intend to marry you with as much pomp and ceremony as I can manage."

"But, Shane—"

"Mother still has a bottle of wine she got the year she and Dad were married. She's been saving it all these years for my wedding. You wouldn't deprive her of that pleasure, would you?"

"Of course not! But—"

"And my sisters'll want to be bridesmaids. And I have a niece just the right age for a flower girl. And a nephew to carry the ring. Speaking of which..." He reached to fumble at the drawer of the night table and produced a small velvet box. "Mother sent this by special messenger yesterday; it's been in the family for years. If you don't like the setting, we'll change it."

Shane opened the box to reveal a beautiful marquise diamond set in delicate white gold. He slid it onto the third finger of her left hand with infinite care and then gently pressed his lips to her hand. "For my bride-to-be," he whispered softly.

Robyn stared dazedly at the lovely ring and then at him. "Shane...it's beautiful." Realizing suddenly that she was being seduced away from the subject at hand, she continued strongly, "But your mother can't—"

"Of course she can." Shane smiled at her. "Mother knows that Marty's all you have. She wants to do this, love."

"You seem to have told her an awful lot," Robyn managed weakly.

"Just that I love you very, very much. She really didn't need to hear any more than that. Will you marry me, witch-lady?"

Robyn stared deeply into his eyes and felt her protests die into silence. "On one condition," she breathed.

"Anything." A slow smile lit his eyes. "If you want the moon, I'll charter a shuttle and go get it."

"Not quite that." She pulled herself forward until she was a single breath away from his lips. "I just want you to put up a mast near the aerie so George'll feel right at home..."

"Hell, darling," Shane muttered thickly, "I'll buy Eric's boat and anchor it in the yard."

It was some time later before Robyn could gather the breath to murmur, "Abracadabra," and wave her hand at the lamp.

The fact that Shane's hand found the switch a moment later, of course, only proved that Robyn wove powerful spells.

New York Times **Bestselling Author**

Nora Roberts

HONEST ILLUSIONS

From carnival tents to the world's greatest stages, Nora Roberts sweeps through the decades to create a shimmering novel of glamorous mystery and intrigue.

"Her stories have fueled the dreams of twenty-five million readers." –Entertainment Weekly

"Move over, Sidney Sheldon: the world has a new master of romantic suspense..." –Rex Reed

"Roberts combines...sizzling sex, a cunning villain, a captivating story, some tugs at the heartstrings–and then adds a twist...and the result is spellbinding."
–Publishers Weekly

___ 0-515-11097-3/$5.99

For Visa, MasterCard and American Express ($15 minimum) orders call: 1-800-631-8571

FOR MAIL ORDERS: CHECK BOOK(S). FILL OUT COUPON. SEND TO:

BERKLEY PUBLISHING GROUP
390 Murray Hill Pkwy., Dept. B
East Rutherford, NJ 07073

NAME————————————————

ADDRESS—————————————

CITY————————————————

STATE ——————— ZIP ———

PLEASE ALLOW 6 WEEKS FOR DELIVERY.
PRICES ARE SUBJECT TO CHANGE WITHOUT NOTICE.

POSTAGE AND HANDLING:
$1.75 for one book, 75¢ for each additional. Do not exceed $5.50.

BOOK TOTAL $ _____

POSTAGE & HANDLING $ _____

APPLICABLE SALES TAX $ _____
(CA, NJ, NY, PA)

TOTAL AMOUNT DUE $ _____

PAYABLE IN US FUNDS.
(No cash orders accepted.)   457

National Bestselling Author
PAMELA MORSI

"I've read all her books and loved every word."
—*Jude Deveraux*

WILD OATS

The last person Cora Briggs expects to see at her door is a fine gentleman like Jedwin Sparrow. After all, her more "respectable" neighbors in Dead Dog, Oklahoma, won't have much to do with a divorcee. She's even more surprised when Jed tells her he's just looking to sow a few wild oats! But instead of getting angry, Cora decides to get even, and makes Jed a little proposition of her own...one that's sure to cause a stir in town–and starts an unexpected commotion in her heart as well.

__0-515-11185-6/$4.99 (On sale September 1993)

GARTERS

Miss Esme Crabb knows sweet talk won't put food on the table–so she's bent on finding a sensible man to marry. Cleavis Rhy seems like a smart choice...so amidst the cracker barrels and jam jars in his general store, Esme makes her move. She doesn't realize that daring to set her sights on someone like Cleavis Rhy will turn the town–and her heart–upside down.

__0-515-10895-2/$4.99

For Visa, MasterCard and American Express ($15 minimum) orders call: 1-800-631-8571

FOR MAIL ORDERS: CHECK BOOK(S). FILL OUT COUPON. SEND TO:

BERKLEY PUBLISHING GROUP
390 Murray Hill Pkwy., Dept. B
East Rutherford, NJ 07073

NAME————————————————

ADDRESS—————————————

CITY——————————————————

STATE ———————— ZIP——————

PLEASE ALLOW 6 WEEKS FOR DELIVERY.
PRICES ARE SUBJECT TO CHANGE WITHOUT NOTICE.

POSTAGE AND HANDLING:
$1.75 for one book, 75¢ for each additional. Do not exceed $5.50.

BOOK TOTAL $ ____

POSTAGE & HANDLING $ ____

APPLICABLE SALES TAX $ ____
(CA, NJ, NY, PA)

TOTAL AMOUNT DUE $ ____

PAYABLE IN US FUNDS.
(No cash orders accepted.)

448

Nationally bestselling author

JILL MARIE LANDIS

___COME SPRING 0-515-10861-8/$4.99
"This is a world-class novel . . . it's fabulous!"
                                    –Bestselling author Linda Lael Miller
She canceled her wedding, longing to explore the wide open West. But nothing could prepare her Bostonian gentility for an adventure that thrust her into the arms of a wild mountain man. . . .

___JADE 0-515-10591-0/$4.95
A determined young woman of exotic beauty returned to San Francisco to unveil the secrets behind her father's death. But her bold venture would lead her to recover a family fortune–and discover a perilous love.

___ROSE 0-515-10346-2/$4.50
"A gentle romance that will warm your soul."–Heartland Critiques
When Rosa set out from Italy to join her husband in Wyoming, little did she know that fate held heartbreak ahead. Suddenly a woman alone, the challenge seemed as vast as the prairies.

___SUNFLOWER 0-515-10659-3/$4.99
"A winning novel!"–Publishers Weekly
Analisa was strong and independent. Caleb had a brutal heritage that challenged every feeling in her heart. Yet their love was as inevitable as the sunrise. . . .

___WILDFLOWER 0-515-10102-8/$5.50
"A delight from start to finish!"–Rendezvous
From the great peaks of the West to the lush seclusion of a Caribbean jungle, Dani and Troy discovered the deepest treasures of the heart.

For Visa, MasterCard and American Express orders ($15 minimum) call: 1-800-631-8571

FOR MAIL ORDERS: CHECK BOOK(S). FILL OUT COUPON. SEND TO:	POSTAGE AND HANDLING: $1.75 for one book, 75¢ for each additional. Do not exceed $5.50.
BERKLEY PUBLISHING GROUP 390 Murray Hill Pkwy., Dept. B East Rutherford, NJ 07073	BOOK TOTAL $ _____
NAME_____	POSTAGE & HANDLING $ _____
ADDRESS_____	APPLICABLE SALES TAX $ _____ (CA, NJ, NY, PA)
CITY_____	TOTAL AMOUNT DUE $ _____
STATE_____ZIP_____	PAYABLE IN US FUNDS.
PLEASE ALLOW 6 WEEKS FOR DELIVERY. PRICES ARE SUBJECT TO CHANGE WITHOUT NOTICE.	(No cash orders accepted.) 310

THE NEW YORK TIMES *BESTSELLING*
***AUTHOR OF* DANIEL'S BRIDE**

LINDA LAEL MILLER

ventures into a scintillating new realm of romance

Forever and the Night

**Senator's aide Neely Wallace can't resist the
erotic charm of reclusive Connecticut millionaire
Aidan Tremayne. As they become closer, Neely
discovers the dark secret that Aidan has been
living with for centuries: he is a vampire, damned
to a bloodthirsty immortality against his will. His
passion for a mortal woman is forbidden. But
temptation stirs the hunger within him...and threat-
ens to destroy them both.**

___ *0-425-14060-1/$5.50 (On sale November 1993)*

For Visa, MasterCard and American Express ($15 minimum) orders call: 1-800-631-8571

FOR MAIL ORDERS: CHECK BOOK(S). FILL
OUT COUPON. SEND TO:

BERKLEY PUBLISHING GROUP
390 Murray Hill Pkwy., Dept. B
East Rutherford, NJ 07073

NAME———————————————————

ADDRESS————————————————

CITY————————————————————

STATE——————————— ZIP————

PLEASE ALLOW 6 WEEKS FOR DELIVERY.
PRICES ARE SUBJECT TO CHANGE WITHOUT NOTICE.

POSTAGE AND HANDLING:
$1.75 for one book, 75¢ for each
additional. Do not exceed $5.50.

BOOK TOTAL $ ____

POSTAGE & HANDLING $ ____

APPLICABLE SALES TAX $ ____
(CA, NJ, NY, PA)

TOTAL AMOUNT DUE $ ____

PAYABLE IN US FUNDS.
(No cash orders accepted.)   **462**